DREAM TEAM

ATTACK OF THE HEEBIE JEEBIES

This book is dedicated to
Sachin and Krishna, stay awesome you two!

First published 2020 by Macmillan Children's Books
an imprint of Pan Macmillan
The Smithson, 6 Briset Street, London EC1M 5NR
Associated companies throughout the world
www.panmacmillan.com

ISBN 978-1-5290-2915-4

1 3 5 7 9 8 6 4 2

A CIP catalogue record for this book is available from the British Library.

Printed and bound in Poland by Dimograf

TOM PERCIVAL

Erika Delgano was in a BAD mood.

Someone had chewed the fingers RIGHT OFF her favourite toy.

Someone had spilt blackcurrant juice ALL OVER her best T-shirt.

And *someone* had cried all the way through the school play, making her FORGET her lines.

This *someone* wasn't just anyone either.

They lived in her house, they had bewitched her parents and she couldn't get away from them, no matter what she did! This *someone* was her brother – Randall.

Admittedly Randall was only just over a year old and probably didn't mean to upset her, but all the same. . . With every day that passed, Erika grew crosser and crosser until she worried she might actually **POP!** Apparently nobody had ever *actually* popped from anger, but Erika was convinced that she would be the first.

Now, to cap it all off, she was stuck upstairs on yet another stupid TIME OUT while everyone else was downstairs, playing happy families.

Erika stomped around her room. When she was fed up with that, she kicked her bedpost. HARD. That hurt her foot, making her even crosser. So she picked up a bouncy ball and hurled it at the wall.

THUMP!

There! That *did* make her feel better (for about 0.3 seconds), until the ball bounced back and hit her on the nose.

Erika wanted to cry. Randall had completely obliterated her picture. He'd even dribbled on it. But was *he* punished? Was *he* sent to his cot for a TIME OUT? *No he wasn't!*

Admittedly, she hadn't spent long on the picture, and she *had* left it on the floor, but still . . . it was *SO* unfair! Or at least that's how it seemed to Erika, but she was forgetting one rather important thing.

When Erika had seen the ruined picture, she'd run in and yelled at Randall, calling him '*A nasty little beast!*' and making him cry. That was the thing about Erika: when she lost her temper – she **REALLY** lost it.

And now here she was . . . Up in her

room with a bruised foot, a sore nose and an unpleasant squirming feeling in her tummy. If she hadn't been so angry, she might have realized that she felt a teeny bit bad about yelling at Randall – but she was still angry.

After a while, Erika heard her mum carrying Randall up to bed. She waited a couple of minutes and then tiptoed downstairs. She imagined having her dad all to herself; perhaps they'd have a game of football in the garden, like they used to . . . *before Randall.*

Erika found her dad in the kitchen. He was fast asleep at the table, his cheek cushioned on a half-eaten sandwich and his hand cradling a cold cup of tea. Drooling.

Erika shuddered – parents could be *really* disgusting sometimes.

'Dad?' she whispered.

No reply.

'Dad,' Erika repeated, more forcefully.

Still no reply.

she shouted in his ear.

'Whaaaa?' yelped Erika's dad, jerking upright and spilling cold tea down his shirt.

'Ah, you're awake,' said Erika innocently.

'Must have dropped off . . .' mumbled Erika's dad, rubbing his face and peeling a slice of cucumber off his cheek. He went to put it in his mouth, but stopped when he noticed Erika's expression. 'I'm just so tired at the moment . . .'

'Really?' interrupted Erika quickly. There was *nothing* worse than hearing your parents bore on about how tired they were, which her parents did. **ALL. THE. TIME.**

Well, they did *now* . . .

'Anyway,' she continued, 'do you fancy a kick-about in the garden?'

'I'd love to . . .' said her dad, wiping a

dollop of mustard from his beard, 'but I'd better get the washing-up done.'

Erika's heart sank; he always *used* to want to play football.

'What about *after* that?'

Erika's dad glanced up at the clock.

'I don't know . . .' he said. 'It's getting late and Randall's been up a lot in the night recently.'

'Mm-hmm,' mumbled Erika. It was pretty much her only response whenever her parents talked about Randall.

'He gets terrible wind, you see,' added her dad.

'Mm-hmm,' muttered Erika.

'Of course, it might be a dairy intolerance . . .'

'Mm-hmm,' growled Erika.

'Either that or a—'

I DON'T

Erika exploded, surprising even herself.

'ALL YOU EVER DO IS TALK ABOUT RANDALL! YOU NEVER ASK ABOUT ME, YOU NEVER WANT TO SPEND TIME WITH ME!

IT'S ALL "RANDALL, RANDALL, RANDALL"!'

She was shouting now.

'I WISH HE WASN'T EVEN HERE!'

For a few seconds she and her dad faced each other in the silent kitchen. There was a loud cry from upstairs then Erika's mum yelled down, '*Great!* You've woken Randall! That's just *perfect*. Thanks a lot.'

Hot tears prickled around Erika's eyes.

'Erika . . .' began her dad. 'I'm sorry. Listen, we can talk about –'

But Erika had gone. She'd pushed past her dad and run through the living room. Speeding upstairs, her feet beat out the rhythm of her thoughts.

IT'S *NOT* FAIR.

IT'S *NOT* FAIR.

IT'S *NOT* FAIR.

Erika barged inside her room and flung the door shut with a slam that shook the walls. She threw herself down on her bed, shoulders heaving with furious sobbing.

Eventually . . .

she fell asleep.

As Erika slept, the anger boiled inside her, twisting her dreams into something **dark** and **cold** – a nightmare.

Erika dreamed that she was back in her kitchen with her family. Her parents were fussing over Randall, just as they did in real life.

'It's always like this, isn't it?' whispered an invisible voice. Erika looked around, but there was nobody there.

'They always take his side, don't they?' hissed the voice.

Erika nodded, blinking back tears.

'How does that make you feel?' asked the voice.

'Angry,' muttered Erika.

'Yes,' comforted the voice. ***'I know... So, give in to your anger, use it as strength.'***

Erika felt a rush of heat swelling up inside her. The voice was right. Her parents were *always* taking Randall's side over hers and it wasn't fair! But she'd show them! Erika felt the heat intensifying, she felt herself give in to the anger . . .

Then a powerful vibration tore through the ground and Erika felt the strangest desire to laugh.

'Nooooooo!' roared the voice in her head – then it vanished. The kitchen scene melted away and Erika found herself standing in a clearing within a forest of rainbow-coloured trees.

A nearby river flowed backwards over a gleaming emerald cliff, in a spectacular reverse waterfall. Above Erika's head, impossibly bright metallic leaves sparkled and glittered in the shimmering light.

This was all very . . . peculiar. The last thing she could remember was the argument at home, then there had been that strange voice and now . . . she was *here* – wherever *here* was. Erika had the strangest sensation that she might be dreaming.

A fish rode past on an old penny-farthing bicycle, wearing a black coat and a large top hat. It nodded politely and said, 'Good day.'

Erika stared at the fish. Since when could they talk, *or* ride bikes? And that was ignoring the fact it was wearing clothes and *wasn't* underwater.

That settled it, thought Erika as the fish pedalled away – she was *definitely* dreaming.

Erika shifted her weight from foot to foot. The ground felt light and springy. When she tentatively hopped up and down, she found that she bounced whole metres into the air. Erika grinned, and after taking a larger jump was catapulted across the whole clearing. She landed on one of the higher branches of a semi-transparent tree, laughing uncontrollably. For a moment she sat there, marvelling at this impossible world, stretching out in all directions.

Just as she was wondering how she would get down, the branches of the tree knitted together into a slide, which

spiralled all the way down the tree trunk, and Erika slid safely to the floor.

'I wish I never had to wake up!' she whispered under her breath, but was distracted by a rustling, snuffling sound behind her. She turned to see it was a small furry creature. Brightly coloured vines were curled and knotted around its arms and legs, binding it tightly to the ground. The sight of Erika's face peering down made it squeal. It was about the size of a large rabbit, or a small dog, or a really *really* big mouse, and it was covered in soft fur. Two little ears poked out of the top of its head and a tail waggled around behind it. It had stubby legs, short arms and a *lot* of pointy little teeth in its wide mouth.

'Heebie Jeebie?' said the creature warily. Erika blinked as she stared at the curious creature, then it spoke again.

'Heebie Jeebie!'

'Sorry...what?' she asked, leaning forward. 'I don't understand.'

'Heebie Jeebie!' came the reply as it wriggled furiously around, but the more it struggled, the tighter the vines became.

'Oh! You're stuck?' Erika reached down and untied the knotted vines. She tried to help the creature up, but it yelped so loudly that Erika panicked and accidentally knocked it over. In return, she was bitten on the arm – *hard*.

'**OWWWWW!**' shrieked Erika. 'You nasty little **BEAST!**'

She looked down at the bite mark on her arm. A strange light glowed around the edges of the wound, but it healed almost instantly and the glow faded away. Strangely, her arm wasn't actually hurting any more, but Erika was still *very* cross.

'What did you do *that* for?' she muttered. 'I was only trying to help, and you BIT ME!'

'Heebie Jeebie . . .' said the creature quietly.

'I don't even care,' growled Erika. 'Just *leave me alone*!'

The creature stared at her, its mouth quivering, large round eyes gleaming with unshed tears.

'Fine! *I'll* go!' Erika turned and stomped briskly away.

She hadn't got far when she felt something tighten round her middle, pulling her backwards. She looked down, feeling her stomach with her hands, but there was nothing there. She walked more forcefully and was able to cover a small distance, but it was slow-going.

A loud wail of

'Heebie Jeebie!'

rang out behind her and the creature burst into tears. She spun around to see it being dragged across the floor, arms and legs waving frantically in the air. She stopped, and it stopped, as though an invisible rope were tied between them. *Somehow* the two of them were connected. Erika scowled – *well this was just perfect*!

The creature sprawled unhappily on the floor, an astonishingly long purple bogey dangling from its nose. This was *exactly* the sort of thing that Randall did – except his bogeys weren't purple. Thinking about her brother gave Erika an idea – whenever he was upset, it was usually to do with either food or sleep. She looked around to find the creature something to eat and saw a tree nearby with tinned pineapples growing on it.

'OK . . .' said Erika, walking over to squat down in front of the creature, 'I'll get you something to eat, but you've got to come along with me.' She placed a hand on his arm. 'And *please* stop crying.'

The creature sniffled and blew its nose on the back of its arm in a loud and disgusting way, but at least it had stopped wailing.

'So. . . do you have a name?' Erika asked.

The creature muttered, '**Heebie Jeebie**,' very quietly.

'Your name is **Heebie Jeebie?**'

The creature shook its head crossly and a speech bubble appeared in the air. It had pictures inside it. A cartoon eye floated next to a mouth, which moved up and down and had pictures coming out of it.

Erika giggled. 'Cool!' she said. 'But . . . what does it *mean*?'

The creature gave Erika a withering look. Once again the speech bubble appeared, but *this* time it just had the mouth and pictures in it. The more she looked at it, the more it looked like the mouth was talking.

'*Talking pictures . . .*' said Erika slowly. 'You *speak* in pictures?'

'Heebie Jeebie,' said the creature sounding much happier, and a nodding head appeared in the speech bubble.

'So what's your name, then?' asked Erika, smiling at the funny little creature.

A speech bubble appeared with an

indecipherable series of squiggles and patterns in it.

'Riiiiiight . . .'

Erika shook her head. 'How about I just call you . . .' She peered more closely at him. **'Beastling?** You look like a **Beastling.'**

The creature shrugged, but didn't seem to disagree.

'OK, **Beastling**,' said Erika. 'So how come you're all alone? Don't you have any friends?'

'Heebie Jeebie . . .' said Beastling sadly, showing a picture of lots of creatures just like him, wandering off and leaving him trapped in the vines.

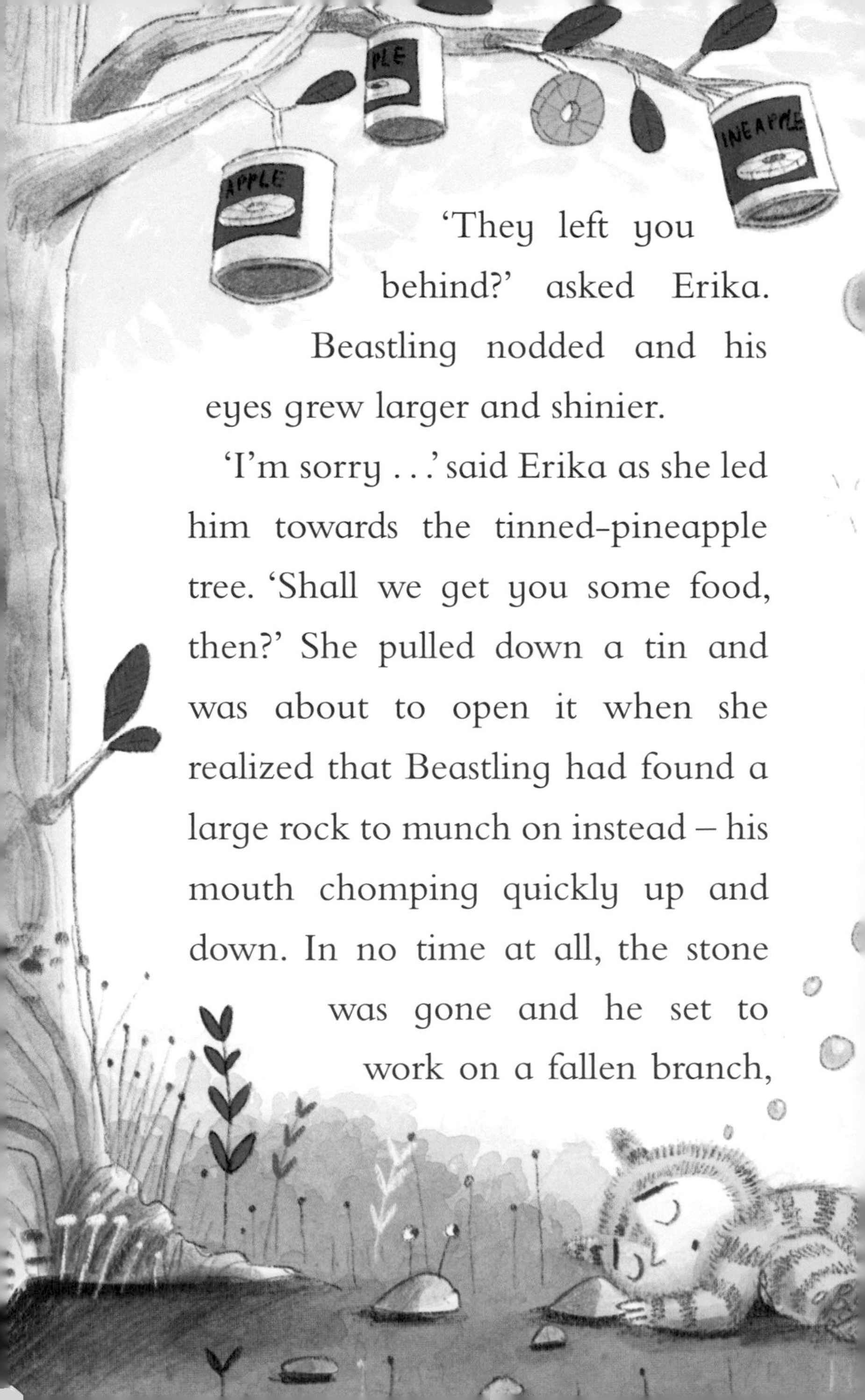

'They left you behind?' asked Erika.

Beastling nodded and his eyes grew larger and shinier.

'I'm sorry . . .' said Erika as she led him towards the tinned-pineapple tree. 'Shall we get you some food, then?' She pulled down a tin and was about to open it when she realized that Beastling had found a large rock to munch on instead – his mouth chomping quickly up and down. In no time at all, the stone was gone and he set to work on a fallen branch, devouring it in seconds.

Erika watched in astonishment. As Beastling ate, a strange glow gleamed from his mouth and once he had eaten all he could – a surprisingly large amount for such a small creature – he yawned and lay down to fall asleep, burping bright bubbles into the air.

Erika scratched her head. If she moved while he was asleep, it would wake him up. He might start wailing again and she was very keen to avoid that! If *only* she had some way of carrying him around with her . . .

With a gentle

pppppptttttt!

a rucksack appeared from nowhere. Erika looked at the bag suspiciously.

Where on earth had it come from? It had lots of little air holes sewn into the fabric and seemed perfect for carrying Beastling. Delighted, she picked up the sleeping creature, placed him in the bag and set off to explore.

Soon Erika came across a clearing where beautiful crystal formations hovered in mid-air, chiming with faint, tinkling melodies, while plants and flowers pulsed and glowed in time with the music.

'Incredible . . .' she whispered under her breath.

As Erika walked on she noticed that some trees had been stripped of all their leaves and a lot of their branches. In some cases, only a gnawed stump was poking up above the ground. It looked like the mess that Beastling had left behind after his snack. There were even places where a large chunk of the ground had been gobbled up too, leaving a blank grey. . . *nothingness*. Erika picked up a stick and threw it towards the nearest patch of grey, but the stick vanished as soon as it made contact.

Something about these voids made Erika feel uneasy, and as she walked on she saw even more of it.

Next to one huge expanse of the greyness, she noticed a remarkably *un*-remarkable structure – a battered old garden shed, with wooden walls and a torn felt roof. It looked *very* ordinary, which immediately made it seem out of place.

Erika frowned. After walking around it

a couple of times to check it was safe, she tentatively opened the door and stepped inside. She saw a collection of old plant pots, a battered deckchair and some garden tools scattered about. She *also* saw a pair of eyes watching her in the gloom. Well, actually *two* pairs of eyes – a pair of pairs of eyes. She could just make out a squat, heavy-looking individual made entirely of lumpy bits of stone, and a boy who looked to be about her size – but any similarity between them ended there. Instead of being solid, he was formed out of purple shadows, which became fainter and fainter as she looked down his body. She couldn't see his feet at all.

Erika's heart thudded in her chest as the shadow boy turned to his companion.

'I think she can see us,' he whispered.

'Nonsense!' exclaimed the stone man, thrusting a small electronic device in the boy's face. 'Look, the readings are all correct.'

'Yes . . .' said the boy slowly, pushing aside the screen, 'but all the same – I think she can see us.'

'Of course she can't,' said the stone man. 'She's only human.'

'I know *that*,' said the boy, 'but still . . .'

'And what *exactly* makes you think that?' asked the stone man irritably.

'Because . . . she's pointing at us,' replied the boy. 'And making a sort of *gasping* sound.'

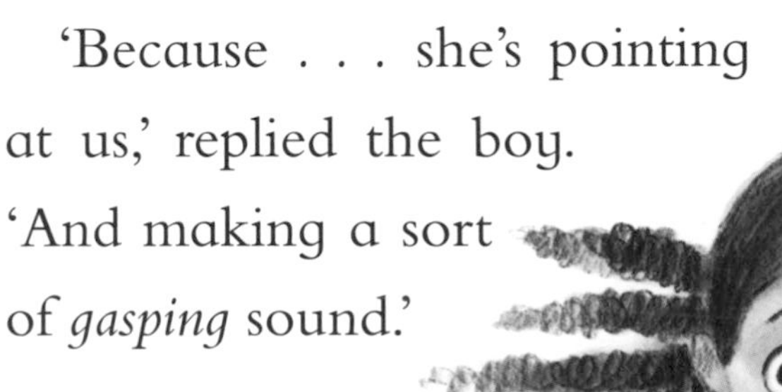

Erika took a step towards the stone man, half scared, but curious despite herself. His head spun round, sounding like two heavy rocks grinding together (because that's exactly what it was). He stood gaping at Erika, who waved and said, 'Er . . . *hello*?'

'She *can* see us!' hissed the stone man out of the corner of his mouth.

'I *know* . . .' whispered the boy, 'but what should we *do* about it?'

'Stay still and do nothing!' muttered

the stone man, fumbling with the buttons on his electronic device. 'I'll make some adjustments . . . The dream will shift and she'll get distracted.'

'I doubt it!' said Erika. 'I mean . . . *whoa* –' A sudden change outside caught her attention – the glowing leaves fell all at once, leaving the trees bare, and it began to snow. Huge snowflakes tumbled gently from the sky and Erika leaned out of the door to catch one of them.

'There!' whispered the gravelly voice. 'She'll soon forget she ever saw us. All we have to do now is wait . . .'

The shadow boy and the stone man glanced at each other, then at Erika, then back to each other again. Nobody moved. Nobody even breathed.

They all stood still,
silently watching each other.

And waiting . . .

And *waiting* . . .

'This is ridiculous!' said the boy. 'She can still *definitely* see us! Why don't we just talk to her?'

'Breaks the rules . . .' grumbled the stone man.

'Oh, I won't tell anyone,' said Erika quickly. 'I promise!'

'Well, you'd better not!' muttered the stone man, glaring at Erika. 'Otherwise there'll be *trouble*!'

Erika took a step back. 'Now look,' she said, her voice trembling, 'if this is going to turn into a nightmare, then I'd much rather just wake up now!'

'You mean . . . you *know* you're dreaming?' asked the stone man weakly.

'Well, *you're* a bit of a giveaway, aren't you?' responded Erika. 'I mean *really*! A lumpy old man made out of stone – it's just silly!'

The stone man bristled. 'It's *not* silly!' he exclaimed. 'A lot *less* silly than being made out of . . . well, whatever it is that *you're* made out of!'

'Let's all just *calm down,* shall we?' said the shadow boy. 'I can sense a bit of tension here.'

'No kidding!' said Erika. She took off the rucksack with Beastling sleeping inside it and folded her arms defiantly.

The boy turned to face her. 'Let's start again . . . My name's Silas and this is Wade.' He indicated the stone man, who said nothing.

'Sorry about Wade,' added Silas. 'He can be a bit grumpy when he's . . . Actually he's *always* a bit grumpy. Anyway, what's *your* name?' He smiled at Erika.

She narrowed her eyes and eventually replied, 'Erika.'

'OK, well, nice to meet you, Erika,' said Silas. 'We're the **DREAM TEAM!** *Ta-da!*' He made a big, dramatic gesture and flung his arms wide. Wade shook his head and glowered at Silas, who slowly lowered his arms. 'Well, we're part of it, anyway . . .'

'The **DREAM TEAM?**' repeated Erika. 'Should I know what that is?'

'Well, *no*!' exclaimed Silas. 'That's *exactly* the point! We're meant to be invisible. The **DREAM TEAM** oversees, protects and polices your dreams. Basically, when anything goes wrong here, we put it right! Do you remember feeling angry when you first started dreaming?'

Erika nodded.

'That's because an ***Angermare*** was after you,' interrupted Wade. 'Nasty creatures – *very* nasty. They track down angry dreamers and make them even angrier, feeding off all the negative emotion. Once they get their claws into you, they just keep making you more and *more* furious, until all that's left is *RAGE*!'

His eyes flared alarmingly as he spoke. 'And when *that's* all burned out –

there's

nothing

left.'

Erika stared at him, her eyes wide. 'You mean . . . you'd be . . . *dead*?'

'Good work, Wade,' said Silas, raising one eyebrow. 'You'll have an Anxietymare in here soon . . .' He turned back to Erika. 'Look, don't worry about it – that's why *we're* here! We got rid of that **Angermare** for you by setting off a class-twelve Joy Bomb. It basically sends out a super-powerful wave of positive emotion that can overwhelm even an **Angermare**. It used up a HUGE amount of

DREAM CRYSTAL, but sometimes these things just have to be done!'

Erika stared at him. 'Is it OK if I just *pretend* to understand what you just said?'

'Sure . . .' replied Silas. 'All you need to know for now is that the **DREAM TEAM** have got your back! So our next job is to track down some other creatures that have been eating your dream and . . .' He suddenly stopped talking.

Erika frowned. 'And . . . *what*?'

Silas was staring out through the door, a horrified expression on his face. Erika turned. The forest appeared to be separating into tiny particles of kaleidoscopic colour, which swirled up into the air, vanishing into a gaping grey blankness.

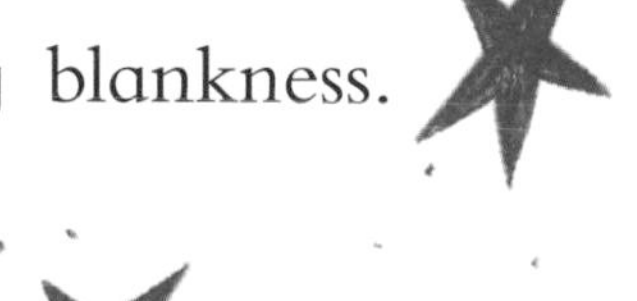

She peered up towards the abyss that opened wider and wider above her.

'The dream's collapsing!' shouted Silas. 'We've got to get out of here! Those **Heebie Jeebies** have eaten so much of the dream that it's falling apart!'

'Who's eaten what now?' asked Erika nervously, thinking about Beastling still asleep in her rucksack. Silas didn't respond but kicked the shed door shut and started adjusting various tools and plant pots. Wade sat down in a broken deckchair, holding a Frisbee and

turning it from left to right as he peered out through the window in front of him, looking for all the world as though he was driving the shed – which apparently he was. Erika gasped as trees shot past the window, speeding up until they were just a blur. Then, in the next moment, there was nothing – no light, no darkness, no *anything*.

CHAPTER 4

There was a burst of colour, sound and sensation, and Erika found that she was no longer standing in a battered old garden shed – she was in some sort of high-tech control room.

'Er, what happened to the shed?' she murmured.

'The shed was a disguise,' explained Silas. '*This* is how we access your dreams– go on, take a look out of the window.'

Erika peered outside. They were speeding along a multicoloured glass tube, which spiralled through an infinitely vast space. Running alongside were countless other tubes, twisting and turning in different directions.

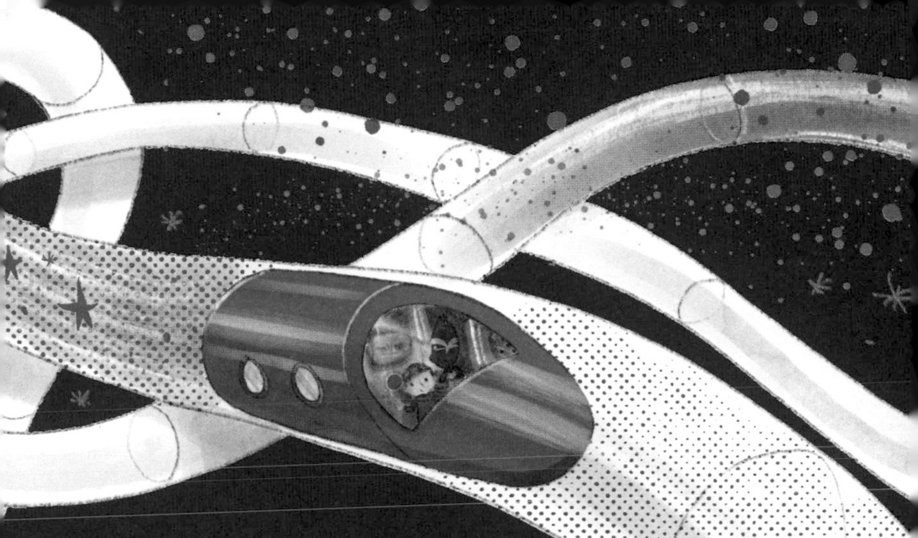

'Wow . . .' she whispered.

'Not something you see every day, right?' said Silas. 'Unless you work in a multicoloured glass spaghetti factory.' He frowned. 'You *don't* work in a multi-coloured glass spaghetti factory, do you?'

'Er, no . . . I go to school,' replied Erika.

'I *thought* so!' exclaimed Silas, then added, 'So I expect you have a few questions about what's just happened?' He glanced over at Erika, but didn't pause long enough to let her actually ask anything. 'OK . . . so *basically* we were searching for the **Heebie Jeebies** in your dream. You might have seen them? They like to eat **DREAM CRYSTAL**, which is what *everything* in your dreams is made of.'

Erika looked over at the bag in which Beastling was sleeping. 'I *think* I saw one of them . . .' she began, but Silas had started talking again – he seemed to talk *a lot*.

'And now *everything's* gone a bit topsy-turvey!' said Silas. 'Your dream's collapsed because the **Heebie Jeebies** have eaten too much of it, and we had to escape!'

'In the shed . . .' said Erika slowly. 'The shed that's actually a space ship?'

'Only the *best* for the **DREAM TEAM!**' said Silas, putting his hands on his hips and winking as he spoke.

'Please don't do that,' said Wade.

'Why not?' asked Silas.

'Because it's *embarrassing*.'

'It is not! It's very *human*. I read it in a book on human behaviour.'

'What was the book called?' asked Wade. '*Embarrassing Human Behaviour You Should Totally Avoid*?'

'You're just jealous that I can do "*human*" so much better than—'

'Hello!' interrupted Erika, waving her hands. 'Can you *please* stay on topic?'

'Of course,' said Silas. 'Sorry. So . . . we had to escape your collapsing dream otherwise you'd have been de-particalized – that means being split apart into the tiniest atoms that make you up. That's actually number seven in the Dreamscape's *Top Ten Most Horrible Ways to Die*, and best avoided if possible. And *now* we need to get back to base, find our boss and try to work out how to get you home.' He smiled expectantly at Erika. 'There, does that all make sense?'

Erika looked up at him. 'OK . . .' she said, a nerve twitching in her lower eyelid. 'I just have *one* question.'

'Go ahead . . .' said Silas.

'What on earth are you talking about?' blurted Erika.

'THIS IS ALL COMPLETELY CRAZY!'

Silas nodded sagely. 'Humans who go through challenging experiences often feel the need to shout to release their emotions – I read *that* in the human behaviour book too. So . . . do you feel better?' he asked.

Erika shook her head.

'Look . . .' she said weakly. 'I think I just want to wake up now.'

'Ah . . .' said Silas slowly. He glanced over at Wade, who pulled a *this-isn't-going-to-go-very-well* sort of face.

Silas sighed. 'You see . . . now that your dream's collapsed you can't actually *go home* – as such.'

'What do you mean, "I can't actually go home – *as such*"?'

Silas looked at Wade again. Wade shrugged in a *you-got-yourself-*

into-this-mess-you-can-get-yourself-out-of-it-too sort of way.

Silas sighed. 'Well, because your dream collapsed, you're disconnected from your sleeping body. Basically... you *can't* wake up at all.' He looked sympathetically at Erica. 'Sorry if I was unclear.'

Erika looked at Silas. She opened her mouth to speak, but no sound came out. Silas patted her on the shoulder.

'Do you want to do some more of that screaming now?'

Erika felt utterly exhausted. She was hopelessly lost, and far away from her home and family. She stared silently out of the window with tears prickling at her eyes as the high-tech pod shot towards **DREAM TEAM HQ**.

Eventually, they came to a stop and a door slid open with a quiet hiss, revealing a vast chamber with hundreds of thousands of stone arches soaring impossibly high overhead. Silas stepped out on to a platform made entirely from glowing beams of light. Wade followed, but Erika hung back uncertainly. When neither of them fell through the ethereal floor, she picked up the rucksack with Beastling inside and followed warily. Row upon row of these platforms ran above and below her, filling the arches with a dazzling fluorescent display of light. There were portals at regular intervals like the one she had just stepped through – countless millions of them.

'And these *all* lead to people's dreams?' asked Erika.

'Pretty much,' replied Silas, 'but not just people. Cats, dogs, dinosaurs – they all have dreams.'

'Sorry . . . did you say *dinosaurs*?'

'Well, yes! Although, to be fair, it's

been a while since there's been an active dinosaur dream in here – how long ago was it again, Wade?'

The stone man glanced at his watch, 'Sixty-six million, two hundred and seventy-five years, three months, nine days and twenty-seven minutes,' he muttered. 'Give or take . . .'

Silas turned back to Erika.

'So yes . . . the Dream Team make sure that *all* creatures have a positive dreaming experience! Anyway . . . welcome to our HQ! What do you think?'

Erika looked around silently.

'Umm . . . extremely odd?' she said eventually.

'Oh. I thought you'd say "*amazing*" or "*fantastic*" or something like that,' said Silas, crestfallen. 'You're the first human to see inside the Dreamscape for around sixty years! This doesn't happen every day, you know!'

'Yeah, and it happened on *our* watch!' added Wade grumpily. 'Have you got *any* idea how much paperwork there's going to be?'

'*Wade* . . .' hissed Silas. 'I think that having to fill in a few forms is preferable to being trapped in an alien world, away from all your friends and family – *OK*?'

'I suppose . . .' muttered Wade, 'but *still*, some of those forms take ages!'

'*ANYWAY*,' cut in Silas abruptly, 'what we need to do now is speak with Madam Hettyforth – if *anyone* knows how to get Erika home, it'll be her.'

He clicked his fingers and in less than a second the glowing platforms, the huge arches and the millions of doorways all vanished, to be replaced by a circular room with one large window. A round table with seven chairs set round it stood in the middle.

'What just happened?' cried Erika, gasping for breath as the world spun in dizzying circles around her.

'Sorry . . .' said Silas.

'I thought I'd speed things up a bit – I should have warned you.'

'Did we just . . . *teleport*?' asked Erika.

'Well, yes!' replied Silas.

'Look at *you*,' muttered Wade, 'showing off your tricks. Did you bother to think about all that **DREAM CRYSTAL** we just wasted?'

'Oh, come on, Wade,' said Silas. 'Our shift's over now – what harm can it do? Anyway, I've summoned the others. They'll be along soon.'

'So what is this **DREAM CRYSTAL** you keep mentioning?' asked Erika.

'It's what fuels everything here,' replied Silas. 'I can move faster than the speed of light, and Wade can transform *anything* that's made of stone, but, to be able to do those things, we need enough **DREAM CRYSTAL**. It's what the whole **DREAM TEAM** runs on. But we can only mine it beyond the Outer Sectors, right next to the Nightmare Zone, and it's *incredibly* difficult to get hold of. That's why we have such strict rations of it. And *that's* why it's so annoying when the **Heebie Jeebies** turn up and eat it all!'

Erika swallowed heavily and glanced around the room. On the tabletop was a bizarre-looking piece of equipment with a glowing screen and a few buttons on it and the walls were covered with posters explaining the risks of **Heebie Jeebies** and

how you should never, *EVER*, in any event, make friends with one.

Erika took off the rucksack and carefully put it down on the floor. She wondered when *might* be a good time to tell the **DREAM TEAM** that she was magically connected to one of their worst enemies. She glanced at Wade's heavy frown and decided that now was not it.

Erika suddenly realized that one place at the table was mysteriously *not* empty any more – a cloud of bright purple gas had appeared in the chair nearest to her.

It turned into a girl who looked *almost* human, except that her clothes, her hair and *everything* about her was exactly the same colour, as though she'd been moulded out of modelling clay. Within seconds she'd morphed into a leopard, then an hourglass and finally a large fish that flopped around uncomfortably on the chair.

'Can you press the "*reset*" button on my collar, please?' the fish asked.

Erika leaned forward gingerly, trying to avoid the slippery scales, and pressed the button, jolting backwards as the girl reappeared.

'Thanks!' said the girl. 'That *always* happens when I meet new people. I get nervous and can't hold on to any one shape . . . and I gabble. Hey, have you ever noticed that when you look *really* closely, all mirrors look like eyeballs? Am I gabbling? I *feel* like I'm gabbling. Just tell me to stop if I'm annoying anyone, because I know that I can be—'

'Stop!' said Silas and Wade at the same time.

'Right. Yes, sorry. I'll stop . . .' said the

girl. She turned to face Erika and smiled. ‘I’m Sim, by the way. Nice to meet you.’

‘Er . . . hi?’ said Erika, too surprised to say much else. She was still gaping at the girl when someone else appeared.

A thickset older woman with a white bun piled up on top of her head was now sitting at the table as well. She was semi-transparent and glowing with a blinding light projected from a large crystal hovering in the air nearby. Everyone nodded towards her, calling out, ‘Ma’am,’ in unison.

‘Right! Let’s not waste any time!’ boomed the lady. ‘Wade, Silas? Can you please explain what the *woolly-word* is going on here?'

'OK,' said Madam Hettyforth, when Wade and Silas had explained everything. 'The good news is that I believe I *can* get you home.' Tears of relief sprang up in Erika's eyes – she *would* see her family again.

'If we can find a compatible dream for you to enter before this Dreamcycle is over,' Madam Hettyforth continued, 'then *theoretically* you should be able to reconnect with your sleeping body. It won't be easy, though. We need to get the dream frequencies perfectly aligned – something only I can do – otherwise you might wake up with your consciousness in a goat's body!'

‘That was an innocent mistake!’ protested Sim. ‘How was I to know it would happen? Besides, we got it all fixed in the end, didn’t we? And the boy suffered no *lasting* damage.’

‘I guess not . . .’ replied Silas. ‘Hey, Erika, you’d know . . . Do humans normally eat their grass off a plate or straight from the lawn?’

Erika’s eyes widened.

Madam Hettyforth reached over and patted her on the arm. ‘Don’t worry, Erika. I’m confident I can do it. But first, we’ve got a bit of time before the end of this Dreamcycle, and I’m curious . . . How could you see Wade and Silas when they were cloaked? That *should* be impossible for humans. It’s not happened since . . .

Well, since it happened to me!'

Erika looked at the bright woman who was projected like a beam of light from a giant crystal. 'You mean *you're* human too?'

'I *was*,' replied Madam Hettyforth, 'but what's important right now, is *you*. Have you ever had a dream like this before?'

'Not as far as I know,' replied Erika.

'So what made *this* dream different?' mused Madam Hettyforth.

'I'm not sure . . .' said Erika uncertainly. *Everything* about this dream was different. But there was one thing it could be . . . She looked up at the posters again, took a deep breath and said, 'It *might* be because Beastling bit me?'

'Because *who* bit you?' grunted Wade.

'Beastling,' continued Erika, sweating ever so slightly. 'I did mean to tell you earlier . . .'

'Tell us what?' growled Wade,

'Wait a minute – I'll wake him up,' said Erika, smiling nervously. She grabbed the backpack from the edge of the room and slowly opened it up.

'Heebie Jeebie?' murmured Beastling, peering around woozily. A large speech bubble with a question mark appeared above his head.

'It's . . . it's . . . *it's a* . . .' stammered Sim.

'Heebie Jeebie!' gasped Beastling, recoiling in terror. Wade leaped forward, swinging a chair at the small creature's furry head. Beastling dodged and sprang around the room in a blind panic while Silas flicked through a self-help book titled *How to Deal with Challenging Circumstances*.

It was hard to see who was more alarmed – Beastling or the **DREAM TEAM**.

Madam Hettyforth pointed a finger towards Beastling and yelled, 'PAUSE!' A trail of bright lights shot out towards the **Heebie Jeebie**, literally freezing him in mid-air.

'So, *this* is the creature that bit you?' asked Madam Hettyforth, breathing heavily as she tucked a stray hair back into her bun.

Erika nodded. 'And *now* we can't be more than a few metres apart!'

Silas whistled between his teeth. 'Well, this is a day of firsts!'

Madam Hettyforth nodded. 'So when you were bitten, some sort of connection must have been forged between you. I've never heard of such a thing happening before, but I wonder if that means you have some other native Dreamscape abilities . . .'

'And *now* we've brought a **Heebie Jeebie** into HQ,' muttered Wade. 'It's going to find our **DREAM CRYSTAL** supplies and eat the lot – I just know it!'

'Calm down, Wade,' said Madam

Hettyforth. 'As long as it's just him, I don't think we'll be in any *real* trouble. But, all the same, let's get this little fellow out of here before any of the others home in on his location. You know what **Heebie Jeebies** are like!'

Just as Madam Hettyforth spoke those words, a **Heebie Jeebie** materialized on top of Wade's head. Another one appeared upside down in the middle of the table, waggling its arms and legs in the air. Then countless other **Heebie Jeebies** began to appear.

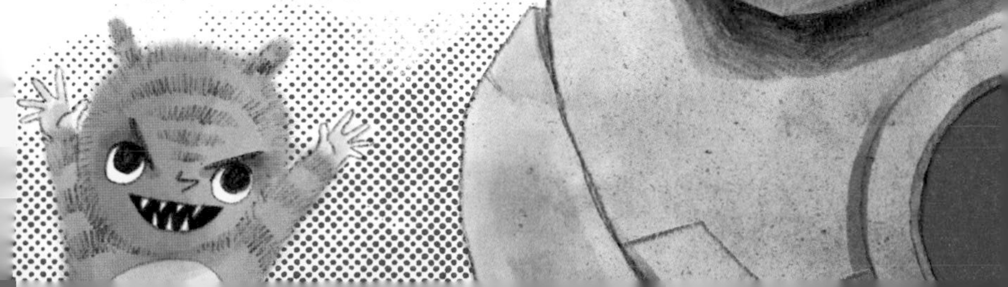

They slid under the door as though they were made out of paper, and rained down from the ceiling – one of them was riding a giant butterfly and wearing a motorcycle helmet, and they were *all* yelling, **'Heebie Jeebie Heebie Jeebie!'**

'Ah . . .' said Madam Hettyforth. 'I think that *now* we might be in *real trouble . . .*'

CHAPTER 6

Within seconds, the room was overrun. There was a massive horde of **Heebie Jeebies** – a flock, a herd, a *whatever-you-call-a-giant-group-of-these-things* of them. They scampered and leaped around while they gnashed their pin-sharp teeth and chanted,

'Heebie Jeebie Heebie Jeebie!'

A group of them dashed over to Beastling, who was slowly beginning to un-pause as the effects of Madam Hettyforth's command wore off. His friends tried to pull him away from Erika, but when they realized that she was being dragged along too they gave up.

Beastling watched his friends abandon their efforts, his eyes wide and shining. He made a speech bubble with his own sad face all alone in it and Erika surprised herself by feeling a bit sorry for him.

Madam Hettyforth dashed over to the device on the table and hurriedly tapped at the keyboard, making a transportation portal appear in the middle of the wall.

Erika stared at Silas as he sped up

and shot past in a blur, racing around the room at impossibly high speeds. Sim was shape-shifting from a tiger to a bear to whichever large, threatening animals she could think of, and helping Silas to drive the **Heebie Jeebies** back towards the transportation portal.

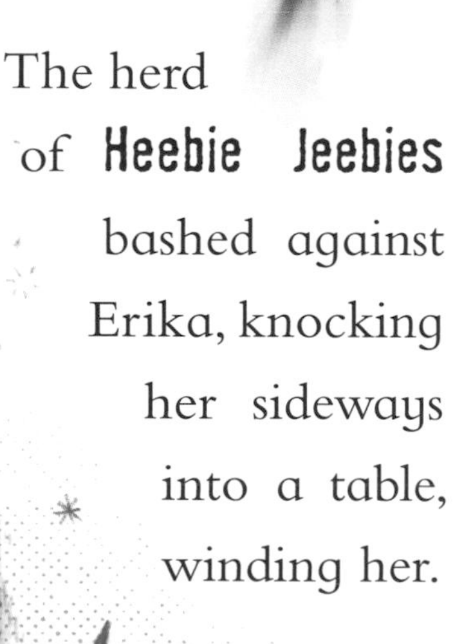

The herd of **Heebie Jeebies** bashed against Erika, knocking her sideways into a table, winding her.

'**WATCH IT!**' gasped Erika, a familiar angry heat returning. She could feel something dark swirling around inside her – something awakening . . .

'Er, Erika? What are you doing?' asked Silas as he sped past.

'*Nothing* . . .' muttered Erika, 'but these furry *idiots* are really starting to get on my nerves!'

'Well, just calm down!' called Wade from the other side of the room. 'Or we might find an Angermare coming for you here – and we do NOT want that!'

'Wade's right,' added Silas, his arms full of wriggling **Heebie Jeebies**. 'Try to calm down otherwise we'll be in a whole world of trouble!'

Erika almost burst with frustration. '**GAH! YOU'RE JUST LIKE MUM AND DAD – ALWAYS TELLING ME WHAT TO DO!**' A surge of energy ran through her. She felt big, strong, powerful and, most of all, **RIGHT**.

'Stop this *now*!' called Madam Hettyforth in a voice as clear as crystal. She gritted her teeth as she raised her arms high in the air and then swept them down, shouting, '**PAUSE!**'

A huge bright flash shot outwards from her, leaving lights dancing behind Erika's eyes for a long time afterwards, and *all* the Heebie Jeebies froze in place.

Madam Hettyforth stumbled sideways and leaned heavily against the table, before she managed to slump into a seat.

'Ma'am?' asked Sim as the **DREAM TEAM** rushed to her side.

'I'm . . . fine . . .' gasped Madam Hettyforth with a wave of her hand. 'Just took more out of me than I expected. It's been a while since I was on active duty!'

Wade's face was even more ashen than usual. It was always ashen because it was made of stone, but *somehow* it became a teeny bit greyer.

'Right!' he barked. 'Silas, Sim, you get this mess cleared up. Just shove them all into the portal – get rid of them.'

'Heebie Jeebie?' asked Beastling, tugging at Erika's arm as he made a speech bubble with the **Heebie Jeebies** being shoved into the portal and a big question mark.

'But where does the portal lead?' asked Erika.

'Does it *matter*?' asked Wade.

'Well, kind of . . .' replied Erika frostily. 'I mean, I know they're annoying, but I wouldn't want them being teleported underwater or anything!'

Wade sighed. 'It leads to the Outer Sectors, OK? So don't worry – they'll be fine. Now *get on with it* while I get Ma'am somewhere safe to rest up. OK?'

Silas nodded and got to work as Wade helped Madam Hettyforth to her feet.

'Wait!' Erika shouted, squinting at a **Heebie Jeebie** that seemed to be watching her. 'I think that one just moved!'

'It can't have,' said Silas. 'They're all paused.'

One of the **Heebie Jeebies** waggled its fingers.

'OK,' said Erika. 'But that one *definitely* moved!'

'Yes . . .' replied Silas, massaging his temples vigorously. 'It did, didn't it?'

The **DREAM TEAM** looked around at each other. With a sudden rush of movement, all the **Heebie Jeebies** came back to life.

Erika watched through the chaos as a huge group of **Heebie Jeebies** swamped Wade and deactivated Madam Hettyforth's projection. The image of the elderly lady flickered and vanished, leaving behind the huge gleaming **DREAM CRYSTAL**.

'You bring her back this *instant*!' shouted Wade, but it was no good. The **Heebie Jeebies** dragged the big crystal towards the door while even more of the furry creatures appeared, flinging themselves at the rest of the **DREAM TEAM** like a solid mountain of fur, teeth and continuous chattering.

'But what do they want?' gasped Erika.

'What they *always* want,' replied Sim. 'To steal as much **DREAM CRYSTAL** as they can – and *apparently* that includes Madam Hettyforth's projection crystal!'

'Can't you do something?' Erika asked, but all anyone else heard was, '*Ham foo goo bumfink*?' because she was buried beneath a huge pile of **Heebie Jeebies**.

Erika felt the seething mass overwhelm her. Flailing and gasping, she fought for air. The chants of **'Heebie Jeebie Heebie Jeebie!'** rang in her ears until it was deafening.

'JUST GET LOST, ALL OF YOU!' she yelled.

The air shimmered and danced around her, crackling with energy. Erika heard a gentle **pppppptttttt!** sound, and then another, then *another* . . . One moment there was a small fluffy bum squashed up against her ear, then with a **pptttttt!** it was gone. Quicker and quicker, the **Heebie Jeebies** began to vanish.

Until they had all disappeared – except one . . .

Beastling, Erika, Silas, Wade and Sim were sprawled around the room. The **Heebie Jeebies** were gone – but so was Madam Hettyforth and her crystal.

'Er, what just happened?' asked Erika.

'Well, the **Heebie Jeebies** have kidnapped Madam Hettyforth!' said Wade. 'I'd have thought even *you* would have been able to see that!'

'But what *happened*?' pressed Erika. 'Where did they go?'

'I think you made them go away . . .' said Silas. 'You made them all get "*lost*" somehow, which is good, but they've *also* taken Madam Hettyforth with them, which is kind of . . .' He winced. 'Bad.'

'But *how*?' asked Erika.

'I really don't know . . .' replied Silas.

'And *I* don't care!' interrupted Wade. 'What *matters* is that we have no idea where those overgrown rats have gone!'

'Well, that's not true, strictly speaking,' said Silas thoughtfully. 'Where do things usually go in the Dreamscape when they're lost or unwanted?'

'You mean . . . the *Barren Zone*?' asked Sim.

'Heebie Jeebie,' gasped Beastling, making a speech bubble filled with a scorching desert scattered with **Heebie Jeebie** bones.

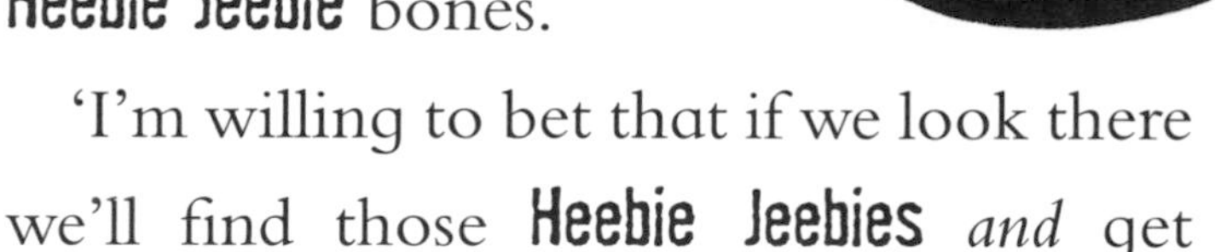

'I'm willing to bet that if we look there we'll find those **Heebie Jeebies** *and* get

Madam Hettyforth's crystal back,' said Silas.

'Well, what are we waiting for?' exclaimed Wade as he ran over to the window and opened it. 'Let's go!'

Erika peered out for the first time since arriving in the room. They were impossibly high up. The wind was tinted with colour and rushed past, leaving curling trails in the air. She gazed around at the vast set of structures that made up the **DREAM TEAM HQ**. A dizzying mass of glowing, semi-transparent buildings spread out almost as far as she could see.

'Come on!' called Sim, nudging past and leaping up on to the windowsill as though she was about to jump out. 'Let's *go*!'

'Are you crazy?' Erika gasped. 'Get down from there – you could fall!'

'That's pretty much the idea,' replied Sim. She leaped outwards for a few metres then began to plummet, very fast, towards the distant ground.

'No!' cried Erika.

'Oh, don't make such a fuss,' muttered Wade. He gave Erika a quick, hard shove and she found herself tumbling out of the window, with Beastling following along behind, screaming, **'Heebie Jeebie!'**

and leaving a trail of speech bubbles filled with his own terrified face.

Churning air rushed past Erika so fast that she could barely even scream. This was *IT*: she was going to die, far away from her home and her family.

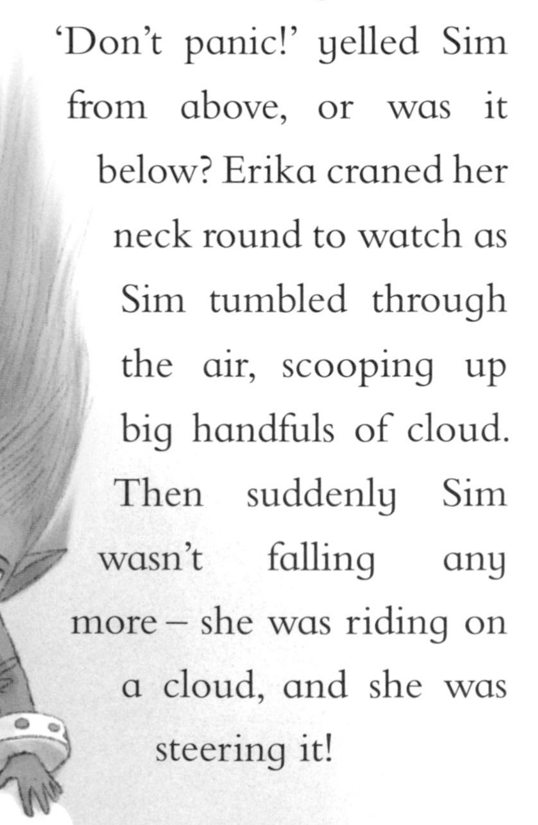

'Don't panic!' yelled Sim from above, or was it below? Erika craned her neck round to watch as Sim tumbled through the air, scooping up big handfuls of cloud. Then suddenly Sim wasn't falling any more – she was riding on a cloud, and she was steering it!

Sim manoeuvred the cloud around until she was riding alongside Erika, who was able to climb on board as well. Then Sim reached out a hand and caught hold of Beastling's tail and thrust him into Erika's lap.

'Hold on tight,' she shouted through the punishing wind. Soon they were soaring up instead of down. The sudden change in trajectory made Erika's stomach lurch and she shut her eyes, waiting for the queasy sensation to pass.

When Erika opened her eyes again, she could see Wade and Silas riding alongside them.

'What *are* these things?' she yelled through the multicoloured wind that rushed towards her.

'Clouds,' shouted Sim. 'Have you ever looked out of the window on a plane and wondered if you could walk on them?'

'Sometimes, yes . . .' Erika admitted.

'Well, here you can!' replied Sim. 'With enough **DREAM CRYSTAL**. Now you'd better get comfy. It's a long ride to the Barren Zone.'

A while later, a sprawling, low-rise city in the middle of a desolate wasteland

came into view. The cloudless sky was a deep, burnt orange, thick with dust particles that stung Erika's skin and made her squint.

'I don't think we're going to make it!' shouted Silas. 'It's too hot – the clouds are evaporating!'

Soon they had dropped to the ground and were skimming the surface of the dry sandy soil at great speed. Erika could feel the cloud shifting beneath her.

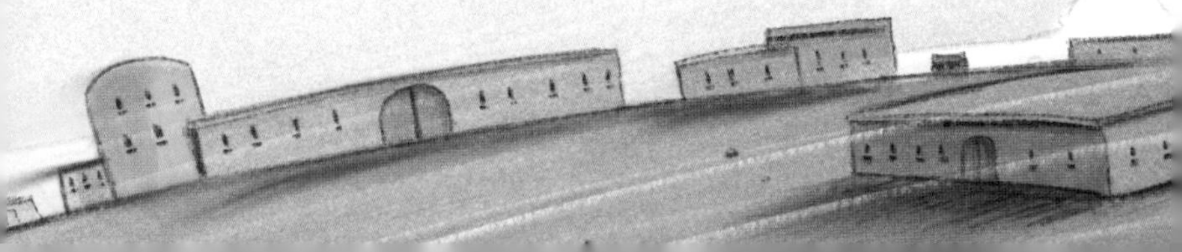

'Get ready to land,' yelled Sim. 'Well… get ready to *crash*!'

Seconds later the cloud evaporated to nothing, and Erika, Sim and Beastling tumbled along the ground.

'Let's hope we don't need to leave here in a hurry,' said Sim as she sat up, beating off huge billows of dusty sand. 'There's not a cloud in the sky – we're certainly not flying out of here!'

'Yeah, and I'm running pretty low on **DREAM CRYSTAL**,' added Wade, inspecting a dial on his wrist. 'How about everyone else?'

'Not so great . . .' replied Sim.

'Me neither,' added Silas. 'Still, we'll just have to make do with what we've got – we've been in worse scrapes before.' He started walking towards the city and the others set off behind him.

'This is the Barren Zone,' Silas explained to Erika as they trudged through the blazing heat. 'It's where things go when they're *truly* lost – including people. Lots of Dreamscape people wind up here when they've done something *really* bad. It's not a very fun place. It's actually number six in the *Top*

Ten Places That You Wouldn't Want to Have a Birthday Party, and number seven is "Inside an Active Volcano".'

Erika swallowed hard as they passed through the gateway leading into the city.

Eventually the **DREAM TEAM** came to a huge market. There were hundreds of stalls packed tightly together. Erika walked past the 'Make Your Own Wishing Well' stall, which basically sold spades, and a wizened old lady selling creased photographs of ice cream that people were walking around licking. The whole place was filled with all sorts of bustling creatures – some humanoid, some animal and some, well . . . some that were just *other*.

Erika's mouth tasted and felt like the inside of an old shoe. An old shoe that had been filled with dirty sawdust from a guinea pig's cage and put inside a baking-hot oven . . . in a house that was on *fire*.

'**Heebie Jeebie** . . .' muttered Beastling, showing a speech bubble filled with a hungry version of himself, looking weak and giddy.

'Not now . . .' whispered Erika. 'We'll get you something to eat soon, though, I promise.'

'Right!' yelled Wade

self-importantly, clambering on to a creaking old table as he puffed out his chest and held up his ID badge. 'Listen up! We're here on *urgent* **DREAM TEAM** business!'

Whatever effect he was hoping to create was spoiled when the table collapsed under his considerable weight and he tumbled to the floor, laughter echoing around the marketplace.

Wade scrambled to his feet, the grey stone on his cheeks giving every impression of turning slightly pink.

'ANYWAY!' he yelled, trying to regain some sense of control. 'We're looking for a large group of **Heebie Jeebies**. Has anyone seen them?'

There were a few muttered exchanges among the shady characters in the square, but they all avoided eye contact with the **DREAM TEAM**.

'Everyone seems very *edgy*,' whispered Erika.

'Yeah,' agreed Sim. 'It's *essential* that we don't do anything to upset anyone!'

'Oi!' yelled a voice from just behind her. 'You with the furry face! Keep your hands *off* me **DREAM CRYSTAL**, or I'll take off your tail with me teeth and make it into a necklace!'

Erika's stomach lurched. *What has Beastling done now?*

She didn't know for sure, but in the two seconds she had to assess the situation she summarized it a bit like this:

Beastling
+
DREAM CRYSTAL
= BIG TROUBLE.

Four seconds later, Beastling, Erika, Wade, Silas and Sim were sprinting down the dusty alleyways of the Barren Zone, chased by a motley assortment of creatures.

'Why are they *all* chasing us?' gasped Erika as the hot desert wind bit at the back of her throat. 'Beastling only upset *one* of them!'

'Boredom probably!' replied Silas, who was running alongside her. 'Just now I saw someone painting a brick grey and charging money to watch it dry. She had a pretty big crowd too – seriously, there is *nothing* to do around here!'

'RAAAAAAARRRARRARRRGHHHHHHH!' roared the crowd behind them, like a living, breathing mass of anger.

'And what will they do if they catch us?' asked Erika.

'Probably cook us and eat us,' replied Silas.

'Or they *might* try to make us eat each

other?' added Sim. 'Or perhaps they'll call us mean things and pull our hair—'

'That doesn't sound so bad,' panted Erika.

'– and *then* try to eat us.'

'Oh.'

Someone in the roaring crowd threw an old boot, which bounced off the back of Erika's head. The sudden sharp pain made her stumble and almost fall to the ground. She winced as she turned to Beastling and yelled, 'It's *your* fault! You're going to get us all *eaten*!'

The anger Erika felt lent her energy and she ran even faster.

'They all just slow you down,' hissed a distant voice inside her head. ***'Spoiling things and telling you what to do. Forget***

about them, forget about all of them.'

The voice was right; she *didn't* care. She didn't care about *anything* any more. All she could feel was the anger – it roared up all around her and she let it consume her.

'Erika!' called Wade. 'You *have* to calm down! *Please!*'

'DON'T TELL ME WHAT TO DO!' replied Erika, red-hot anger burning in her stomach.

'ANGERMARE!' yelled Sim. 'Coming up right behind us!'

'So fast,' hissed the voice, louder now. ***'No one can catch you!'***

Erika smiled as she ran faster than she ever had before. She felt immensely strong – *powerful.* Beastling tripped and fell, but Erika didn't slow down.

She didn't even care when he cried out – she just carried on running with the **Heebie Jeebie** bouncing along behind her.

Wade bent down to scoop Beastling up and powered along after her, his stone legs pounding heavily into the ground.

Erika wondered why she was still running; she wasn't scared of the Angermare – it was *helping* her. She had no reason to be afraid. She stopped and turned – *there it was*.

It was hard to tell what it was made of – it looked as though it had been scratched out of the world with a jagged stick, revealing a terrible darkness.

It was huge, uncontrollable and terrifyingly powerful.

As she stared up, Erika recognized the creature. It was *her* anger and it was growing. Erika felt as though she could rip the roof off a house, destroy a whole street, a whole city – the whole *world*.

'**Yessss!**' roared the voice in her head. '**Do it! DO IT!**'

'Erika!' gasped Wade. '*Run!* Come on, we've got to get you out of here!'

'WHY?' yelled Erika, fury coursing through her. 'So you can all keep telling me what to do? She glared at Wade, full of hatred and anger.

'I HATE YOU! ALL OF YOU! JUST LEAVE ME ALONE!'

she shrieked, her voice a hideous, grating roar. The anger grew, wilder, stronger and more ferocious until all she felt was rage.

Then suddenly it subsided. Erika's legs weakened, a sickening feeling flooded through her and she stumbled to her knees. A granite arm grabbed her round the middle and Wade carried her down a narrow side street.

'It had you,' he said gruffly. 'Don't worry – could happen to anyone . . . Now, we've got to find a place to hide and stay out of trouble until this blows over.' He glared at Beastling. 'Got it?'

Beastling smiled weakly and a speech bubble with a 'thumbs-up' appeared. Wade used his electronic device to open a rusty old door and they all crept in.

'We'll hide in here,' he whispered. 'Silas and Sim will be fine. We'll catch up with them afterwards.' He placed Erika on the floor of the small cellar and then locked the door. Erika sat down shakily, still not entirely trusting her legs.

'Hey, Erika,' said Wade gently. 'Listen, I know what it's like to feel angry, but you see one of *them* and it's a good reminder to keep things in check. You know what I mean?'

'It was . . . *terrible*,' muttered Erika.

'Yeah.' Wade nodded in agreement. 'But don't worry – we're safe from it here. I put an emotional shield around us when I grabbed you earlier. *Nothing* will be able to read your feelings in here.'

'Thanks,' said Erika quietly.

'It's nothing,' replied Wade. 'Now just *try* to relax, OK?'

Erika nodded, but her thoughts were spiralling out of control. Had she brought that *thing* upon them? Perhaps she *was* out of control? What if it was all her fault? What if she *never* got home? What if she never saw her family again?

As Erika sat in the dark cellar, these troubling thoughts circled like sharks in an ocean – waiting for the moment to attack.

'Hey!' a voice called out. 'Open up. We know you're in there.'

Erika's eyes widened as the lock turned and the iron door swung open to reveal Silas's smiling face.

'All clear!' he said. 'But I tell you what, that **Angermare** hung around for *ages*. I've never seen one do that before, especially when there was so much anger in the crowd for it to feed off – *weird*.'

'Why does it want *me* so much?' asked Erika.

Silas shrugged. 'Sometimes they get quite refined tastes. You know how some humans like raspberry-ripple flavour ice cream and some prefer mince-choc-chip flavour?'

'Or *mint* choc chip,' corrected Erika.

'Exactly!' said Silas. 'Some people like *mince* choc chip, some like *mint* choc chip – it takes all sorts. It's like that with the **Angermares**. Sometimes they just want a particular taste. Anyway, it's left the Barren Zone now, but so have the **Heebie Jeebies**. Still, Sim's managed to work out what direction they left in.'

'Four hundred **Heebie Jeebie** footprints aren't exactly hard to miss!' said Sim, smiling. 'The other good news is that I've sorted out some transportation.

I found an old car. *Well*, I borrowed an old car . . . Well, I kind of *stole* an old car, but I did leave a note and I will bring it back after we've rescued Madam Hettyforth, so *technically* it is borrowing.'

'And what about the angry mob?' asked Wade.

'You know how everyone's *really* bored here?' replied Silas.

Wade nodded.

'Well, I had a few old books with me – one of them was *101 Things to Do Before You're Nine and Seven-Eighths*. So they're all running around trying to find leaves that look like faces. They're going to struggle because there aren't any trees growing here, but still . . .'

Wade frowned. 'OK, so I'm *really*

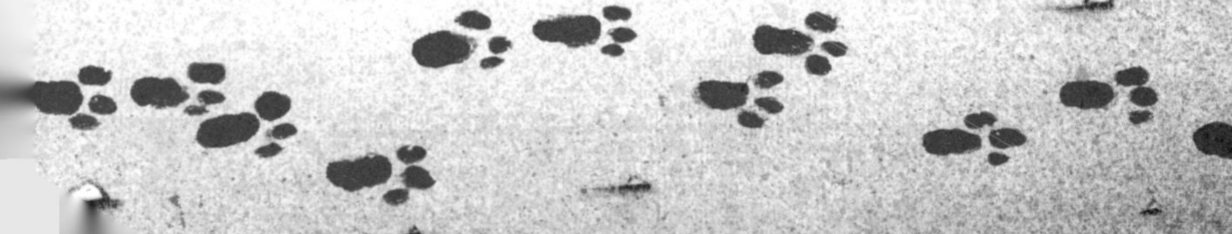

low on **DREAM CRYSTAL**. I used up a lot keeping us hidden from the *Angermare*. Do you think we should go back to HQ and get some more?'

'There's no time!' said Sim. 'If we don't hurry, there won't *be* any Madam Hettyforth left to rescue! Besides the Dreamcycle's nearly over and we need to get Erika home or she'll be trapped here. Look, we'll be fine, as long as nobody *accidentally* eats all of our remaining **DREAM CRYSTAL** . . .'

She gave a long, very hard look at Beastling, who shuffled uncomfortably and muttered, 'Heebie Jeebie,' very quietly. A picture appeared showing himself eating **DREAM CRYSTAL** with a cross through it.

‘That’s good enough for me!’ said Silas. ‘Now, come on, let’s get out of here.’

The **DREAM TEAM** tore across the desert, huddled up in what you could only charitably refer to as a car. It was more like a collection of spare parts that vaguely resembled a car. One of the wheels even looked like a scribbled circle, which someone had drawn in crayon – *badly*.

'So does anyone have any ideas about how to get Madam Hettyforth back?' called Wade from the driver's seat.

It turned out that there were *lots* of ideas – the trouble was that most of them came from Sim, and none were any good.

'I've got it!' she cried. 'So . . . we go back in time *before* the **Heebie Jeebies** appeared and team up with our past selves! ***BOOM!*** Madam Hettyforth never gets taken!'

'That is *SO* cool!' gasped Erika. 'I had no idea you could time travel!'

'There's just one problem,' said Wade slowly. 'We *can't* time travel. Unless someone's invented a time machine and not told us about it!'

'Aha!' said Sim. 'But there *might* be

one . . . *in the future*!'

'OK,' said Wade, grinding his heavy stone teeth, 'can you see any time machines here?'

'No,' said Sim. 'I suppose not.'

'So let's just stick to plans that are *actually* possible – OK?'

'OK . . .' muttered Sim, scowling.

'First things first,' said Wade. 'We need to locate the **Heebie Jeebie** base.'

Sim opened her mouth and Wade growled, 'Sensible, realistic and practical ideas *ONLY*!'

'Heebie Jeebie!' cried Beastling enthusiastically.

'Not now, Beastling!' whispered Silas.

'Heebie Jeebie!' repeated Beastling more insistently.

'Be quiet!' Silas clamped one hand over Beastling's mouth. 'This is serious!'

Beastling shook his head and yelped a muffled, **'HEEBIE JEEBIE!'** A speech bubble filled the car, showing a detailed map of the Dreamscape that marked exactly where the **Heebie Jeebie's** base was. It was a complex network of caves, reaching far beneath the ground, deep in the Outer Sectors.

'Ah . . .' said Silas, slowly moving his hand from Beastling's mouth. 'Of course you'd know where it is . . . Sorry about that!'

Beastling scowled but cheered up when Silas passed him a small **DREAM CRYSTAL** to munch on.

Erika studied the map closely. 'But what does *that* mean?' she asked, pointing to a section of the map which was scribbled out, swirling with coarse, angry marks.

'That's the Nightmare Zone,' replied Silas. 'It's unmapped because no one has *ever* returned from there.'

'Why do the **Heebie Jeebies** live so close to it, then?' asked Erika.

'They're the only creatures in the Dreamscape that aren't affected by the **Angermares**,' explained Wade. 'Or the Anxietymares, or *any* of the Nightmares. Anyway, now that we know where to go, we just need to work out what to do! Any ideas?'

'OK!' exclaimed Sim. 'So—'

'Any *other* ideas?' interrupted Wade firmly.

CHAPTER 10

The cave walls glowed in a dizzying array of colours. Stalactites clung to the ceiling and stalagmites thrust up from the rough stone floor. There were even a few stalag-rights growing sideways across the caverns, but no stalag-lefts anywhere.

'Shh!' hissed Silas. '**Heebie Jeebies** approaching. Everybody out of the way!' Erika, Sim, Silas and Beastling scrambled easily up the walls.

'I *knew* this was a BAD idea!' muttered Wade, whose physique lent itself more to knocking walls down than climbing up them. He sucked in his huge chest as much as he could and the **Heebie Jeebies** passed by without noticing him. Wade, Silas and Sim had combined all of their last remaining **DREAM CRYSTAL** and Silas was using it to create a cloaking shield, which made the group invisible and inaudible – unfortunately it didn't do anything about smells . . .

As the **Heebie Jeebies** jostled past, one wrinkled up its nose and grimaced.

'Heebie Jeebie!' A speech bubble appeared, showing a bird breathing in a noxious cloud of green gas and then falling off its perch – dead.

The **Heebie Jeebies** had a brief but intense argument about who was to blame for the smell. In the end they all seemed to agree that a small ragged member of their party with long tufty ears had been the culprit, and walked away down the tunnel.

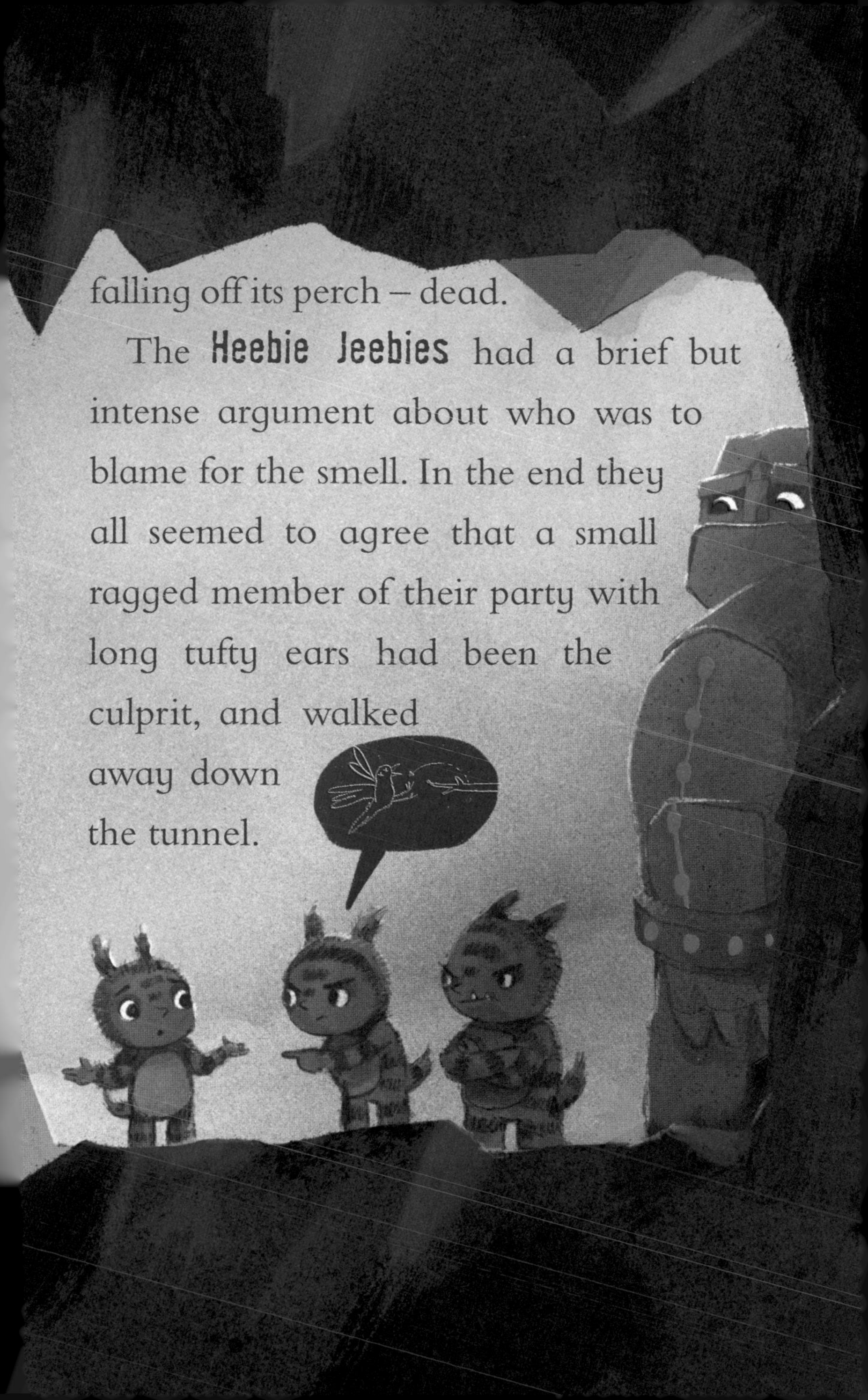

'Who was *that*?' hissed Silas.

'Sorry . . .' muttered Sim, clambering down from the wall. 'It just *happens* when I get nervous – I can't help it.'

'Well, *try*!' added Wade. 'And *also* . . . what have you been eating – rotten eggs and cabbage pie? Seriously, you need to see a doctor when we get back to base.'

'*If* we get back to base . . .' said Silas, looking down at a timer on his wrist. 'Come on now, *focus*! We've got ten minutes of invisibility left to find Madam Hettyforth and get out of here, before the **DREAM CRYSTAL** runs out. Now, Beastling, are you *sure* they'll be keeping Madam Hettyforth's crystal in the central chamber?'

Beastling spun round quickly and

swallowed, burping up a small fizzing bubble.

'Heebie Jeebie!' he replied, slightly defensively, and a map of the caves appeared, showing that they were now very close to a central chamber, which held the huge stockpile of DREAM CRYSTAL that fed the entire community.

'OK, great!' replied Silas. 'Let's keep moving.'

Before long, Erika was peering into a gargantuan multicoloured grotto. There were Heebie Jeebies *everywhere* – climbing up the walls, lying in hammocks, swinging from ropes or just helping themselves to the glittering DREAM CRYSTAL, which flowed out of cobbled-together taps.

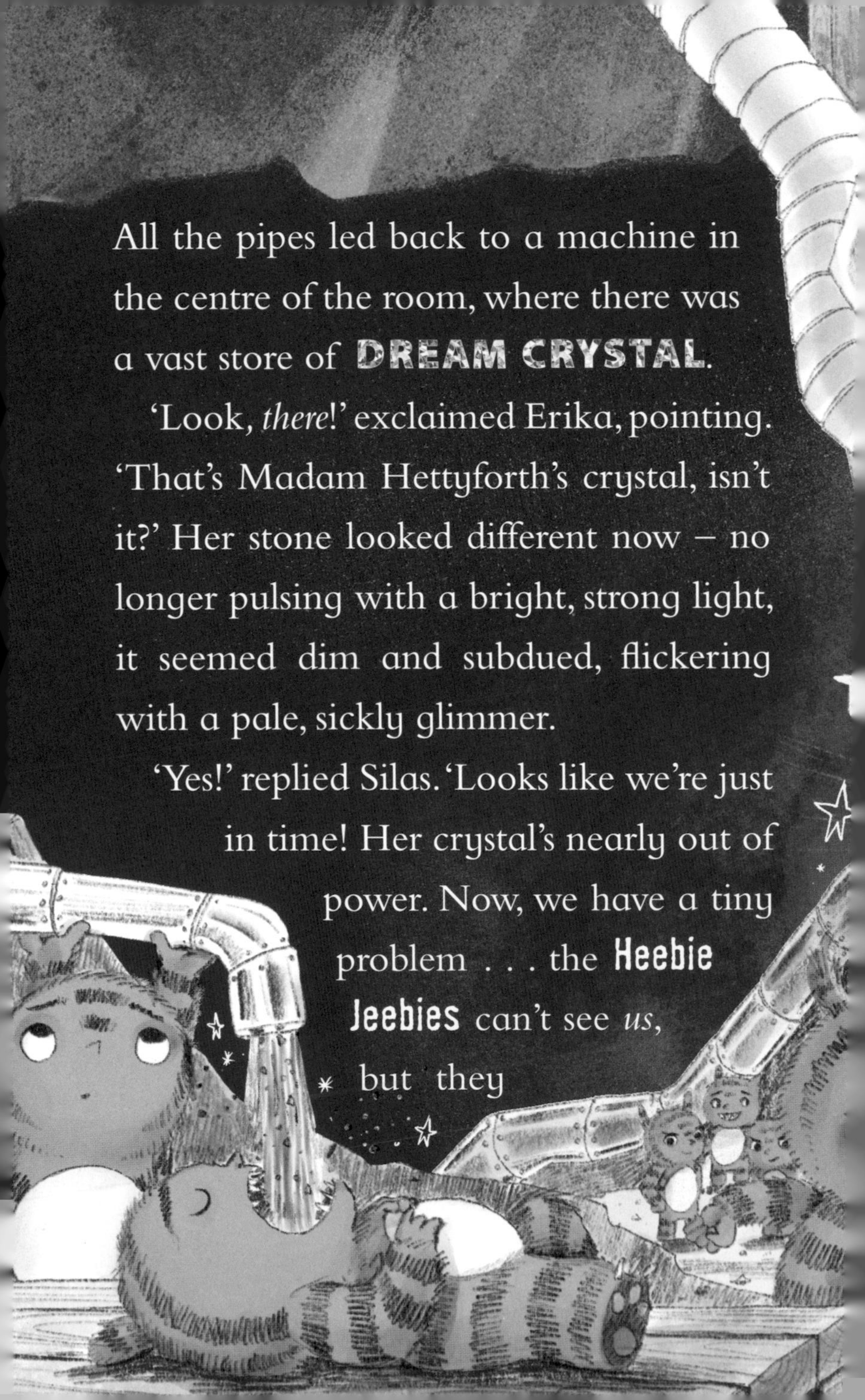

All the pipes led back to a machine in the centre of the room, where there was a vast store of **DREAM CRYSTAL**.

'Look, *there*!' exclaimed Erika, pointing. 'That's Madam Hettyforth's crystal, isn't it?' Her stone looked different now – no longer pulsing with a bright, strong light, it seemed dim and subdued, flickering with a pale, sickly glimmer.

'Yes!' replied Silas. 'Looks like we're just in time! Her crystal's nearly out of power. Now, we have a tiny problem . . . the **Heebie Jeebies** can't see *us*, but they

might notice if Madam Hettyforth's crystal disappears.'

'I've got an idea!' said Erika. 'Can we get the taps to push out *more* **DREAM CRYSTAL** around the cavern?

The **Heebie Jeebies** are so greedy that hopefully they'll be distracted and won't notice what we're doing.'

'Brilliant!' said Silas. 'Sim, you go and increase the output of **DREAM CRYSTAL** while we sneak over to get Ma'am's crystal.'

'Should we, er, "*borrow*" some more **DREAM CRYSTAL** ourselves?' asked Erika.

'It's too risky,' replied Silas. 'If one of them feels us brushing against them, they'll get suspicious! We'll have to make do with what we've got. So, is everyone clear?'

They all nodded, then Sim ran towards the machine in the centre of the room, dodging and weaving through the mass of **Heebie Jeebies**. Once she was there, she pulled a spanner out of her hair and made a few adjustments to the machine. Soon, the taps were spewing out more **DREAM CRYSTAL** into the cavern than the **Heebie Jeebies** could possibly eat. The furry creatures scrambled around excitedly, all trying to stuff in as much as they could.

'Now!' whispered Silas. They ran forward, and Erika and Wade grabbed Madam Hettyforth's crystal while Silas activated her projection. With a jolting flicker, Madam Hettyforth reappeared in the hall.

'What the *woolly-word*—' she gasped, falling to her knees.

'Shh!' whispered Silas. 'Save your energy – I'll explain what's happening later.' He turned to face Wade. 'Can you carry the crystal?'

Wade nodded and soon they were heading back towards the tunnel through which they had arrived.

'Just look at them!' Sim exclaimed as the **Heebie Jeebies** scrabbled around, gobbling up **DREAM CRYSTAL** from the floor. 'So *greedy*!'

One of the **Heebie Jeebie's** ears pricked up. It sniffed at the air suspiciously.

'Er, what's that one doing?' asked Erika.

More and more **Heebie Jeebies** were now looking in their general direction, squinting and straining their ears.

'It's like they can hear us!' she continued, her stomach lurching.

'Not possible . . .' replied Wade. 'We've still got enough **DREAM CRYSTAL** for at *least* five more minutes of cloaking, right, Silas?'

Silas nodded, then looked down at the timer on his wrist and his mouth hung open.

'What?' he muttered, tapping at the timer frantically. 'That can't be right! We've only got . . . five *seconds* of cloaking left!'

As Silas spoke, it became obvious that the **Heebie Jeebies** could now both see *and* hear them. There was a low, throaty growl, and then with a furious roar of

'**HEEBIE JEEBIES**' they sprang forward.

'But what happened?' asked Erika. 'How did we run out of time so quickly?' Then she saw something that made her stomach stop lurching and instead solidify into a cold, hard fury. Beastling was standing right behind Silas, popping the last tiny grain of **DREAM CRYSTAL** into his mouth, a florescent glow glimmering around his lips.

'How could you!' she yelled at Beastling. 'You stupid furry fuzzball! You ate all of our supplies!'

'**Heebie Jeebie** . . .' he whimpered apologetically, but there was no time to see what was in the speech bubble he made. Half a second later, the **DREAM TEAM** were buried beneath a mass of furious **Heebie Jeebies**.

CHAPTER 11

Erika had never felt such rage. It surged through her in overwhelming waves, each crashing, foaming torrent of anger more powerful than the last. She wanted to lash out, to destroy . . . *Anything* to unleash the fury she felt.

'YOU'VE RUINED EVERYTHING!' she yelled. **'NOW I'LL NEVER GET HOME!'**

She was a furious beacon of anger, blazing with an intense heat.

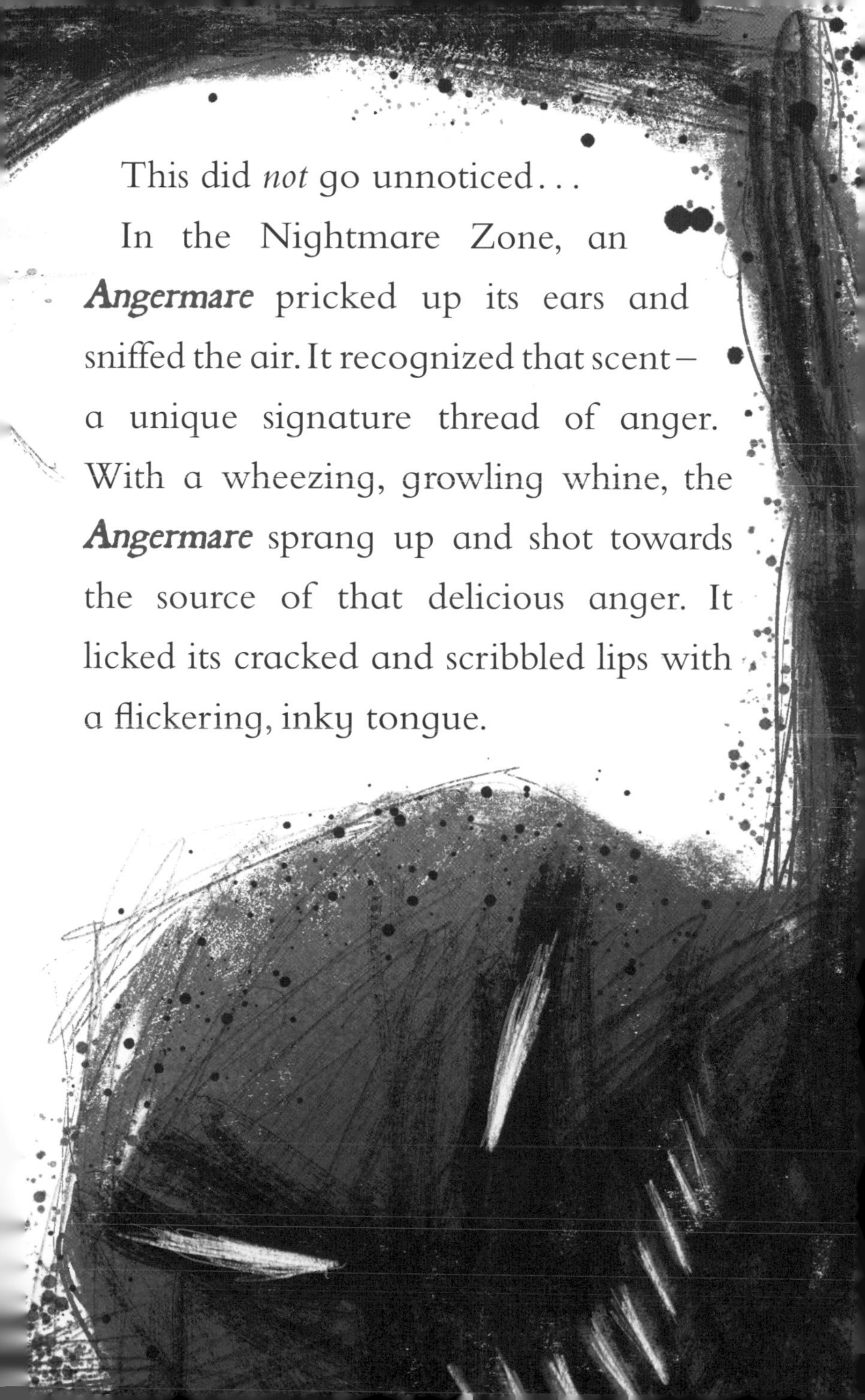

This did *not* go unnoticed...

In the Nightmare Zone, an ***Angermare*** pricked up its ears and sniffed the air. It recognized that scent – a unique signature thread of anger. With a wheezing, growling whine, the ***Angermare*** sprang up and shot towards the source of that delicious anger. It licked its cracked and scribbled lips with a flickering, inky tongue.

Without any **DREAM CRYSTAL**, the **DREAM TEAM** were unable to hold off the **Heebie Jeebies** – there were just *too* many of them. Wade, Silas, Sim and Madam Hettyforth were all dragged off in separate directions. Soon only Erika and Beastling were left, surrounded by hundreds of angry, chanting creatures.

The assembled crowd fell silent as a tall, thin **Heebie Jeebie** tottered over. It wore a long, thick cloak and a bizarre crown with antlers on it. It was clear that this was the leader.

It glared at Erika and poked her on the nose. As it did so, the cloak separated slightly. Erika could *now* see that it was so tall because it was sitting on two other **Heebie Jeebies**, which were puffing and panting away beneath the cloak. The leader took a deep breath and yelled,

'Heebie Jeebie!'

making a speech bubble appear. Erika had no idea what the strange pictures and symbols meant – but it *seemed* like they were insulting her.

'Oh, *whatever*!' she growled. 'Like I care what you *furballs* think!'

At their leader's command, the **Heebie Jeebies** tried to separate Erika from Beastling, but none of their crude efforts worked. In the end, they gave up and locked Erika in a small wooden cage, which rolled around after Beastling wherever he went.

Erika slumped awkwardly in the cramped prison – trapped and helpless. This was it . . . she'd failed. She would *never* get home. She would *never* see her family again.

The thought cut through Erika like a jagged, rusty blade and her anger morphed into frustration and sadness. She didn't even try to hold back the tears that poured down her face. She thought of the last time she'd seen her family – she'd been *so* horrible. She remembered yelling at Randall. She pictured his eager face, gazing up at her, all innocence and enthusiasm – he didn't understand he had done anything wrong – he was *so* young! How could she have yelled at him like that? As Erika sobbed into her grubby hands, the thoughts spun around in her head. Now she would *never* get the chance to say sorry.

But there was one person she could say sorry to – well, one *thing* . . .

'Beastling?' she said slowly. The furry creature didn't turn round, but Erika could tell he was listening.

'I'm sorry . . .' said Erika. 'I was . . . *not very nice*. I shouldn't have shouted at you earlier.'

Beastling slowly turned to face her. He looked Erika straight in the eye and said, **'Heebie Jeebie?'**

A speech bubble appeared with a picture of Beastling next to an equals sign and on the other side of that a very silly-looking ball of fur and a question mark.

Erika smiled slightly. 'No, you're *not* a stupid furry fuzzball. I'm sorry I said that too.' Beastling looked at her, a conflicting range of emotions flickering across his face.

'So . . . are we friends again?' asked Erika. Beastling looked at her a while longer, still unsure. Erika slid her hand out through a gap in the cage and was relieved to feel Beastling's small, furry paw.

'**Heebie Jeebie** . . .' he said quietly. There was an image of Beastling eating lots of

DREAM CRYSTAL and a big plus sign, then a picture of Erika locked in the cage, followed by an equals sign and a very sorry-looking Beastling.

'*You're* sorry?' asked Erika. Beastling nodded.

'That's OK,' said Erika. 'We all make mistakes. I guess what matters is how we learn from them.'

Beastling squeezed her hand and she squeezed back.

The moment was spoilt when a distant, muffled but completely horrendous roar echoed down the tunnels.

All the colour drained from Beastling's face.

'What?' asked Erika. 'What is it?'

'Heebie Jeebie...' whispered Beastling, his eyes huge and round. In the speech bubble appeared an image that Erika recognized all too well – something huge, scribbled, furious and devastating – an ***Angermare***.

Beastling scrabbled at the locks on the cage, but he didn't have a key and couldn't get them open.

On the floor just outside the cage Erika could see a small pile of **DREAM CRYSTAL**. Her heart leaped–

it was in reach. Then she noticed that Beastling had seen it too – it was pretty obvious what would happen next . . .

But Beastling *didn't* gobble up the **DREAM CRYSTAL**. He picked it up and held it out to her. Erika stood there for a moment, staring at him in disbelief. A group of armoured **Heebie Jeebies** dashed past, towards the tunnel where the ***Angermare*** was approaching. One of them swiped out a paw and grabbed the **DREAM CRYSTAL** that Beastling was holding and swallowed it in one gulp.

Beastling's face crumpled and he wailed. He turned away from Erika, his speech bubble filled with pictures that all said 'Sorry!' in a multitude of different ways.

But Erika wasn't cross – in fact she was smiling.

Cogs were turning in her brain, not *real* cogs of course – her brain didn't have any cogs in it – but she *was* thinking hard.

Beastling had shared! Well, he had tried to. Why couldn't they all share? Why couldn't the **DREAM TEAM** *and the* **Heebie Jeebies** *work together?*

'Beastling!' called Erika. 'Listen, I've got an idea! **Heebie Jeebies** eat **DREAM CRYSTAL**, right?'

Beastling nodded.

'But it gets you in trouble with the **DREAM TEAM**, because *they* mine the **DREAM CRYSTAL**, right?'

Again, Beastling nodded.

'And **DREAM CRYSTAL** can *only*

be mined near where the Nightmares live, which makes it hard for the **DREAM TEAM** to get it, but *that* wouldn't be a problem for you because the Nightmares don't affect you, do they?'

Beastling shook his head hesitantly, but looked as though he had just been asked to invent a pencil that a donkey could use.

'So . . .' continued Erika triumphantly, 'why don't we all work as a team? The **DREAM TEAM** and the **Heebie Jeebies** could mine the crystal *together* and share what they find! It's a win-win situation!' Beastling nodded again, his face brightening.

'What do you think?' asked Erika. 'If the **Heebie Jeebies** let the **DREAM TEAM** go, then we can all team up to fight off the **Angermare**!'

'**Heebie Jeebie!**' yelled Beastling. In his speech bubble were an ear and a very well-behaved eye next to a deer.

Erika frowned.

'Sounds like . . .' she said slowly, peering at the pictures. Beastling nodded encouragingly. 'Sounds like . . . *a good eye . . . deer* – a good idea!'

Beastling whooped and grinned at her, then sprinted off to find the chief **Heebie Jeebie** to explain the plan, with Erika rattling along in the cage behind him.

CHAPTER 12

'Seriously though,' said Wade, glaring at the **Heebie Jeebies** helping Madam Hettyforth out of a cage. 'How did you get them to set us free?'

'I'll explain later,' replied Erika. 'First we've got to get rid of the ***Angermare***. Have you all been given more **DREAM CRYSTAL**?'

Everyone nodded. Madam Hettyforth was back to her full height and once again shining with a dazzling luminescence.

'I can't say I *really* understand any of

this,' said the elderly lady, 'but *well done*, Erika!'

'And Beastling!' said Erika. 'It was because of him that we got the other **Heebie Jeebies** on board!' She bent down and ruffled Beastling's fur.

'Now, listen!' called Madam Hettyforth. 'We've never faced an ***Angermare*** as powerful as this one – we've got to be on top of our game here. OK?'

'Yes, Ma'am!' chorused the **DREAM TEAM**.

'So let's get out there and give that fiend what for! Everybody ready?' There was a loud cheer from the assembled **Heebie Jeebies**. Their leader was mounted on a huge black stallion, holding a shiny shield and a spear. The stallion was just another two **Heebie Jeebies** dressed up like a horse, but, as far as the assembled crowds were concerned, this was their glorious leader, ready to lead them into battle.

'CHARGE!' yelled Madam Hettyforth, and they all raced down the tunnels towards the fast-approaching ***Angermare***.

It was the first time that Erika had *really* been able to see what the **DREAM TEAM** were capable of. With a full charge of **DREAM CRYSTAL**, they were unstoppable – there was *nothing* they couldn't do. Silas sped up his movements and shot towards the ***Angermare***, a dizzying purple blur. Sim shape-shifted into a hummingbird and

darted down the corridor, but when the **Angermare** threw a boulder towards her she changed into a diamond bullet and shot straight through the huge rock, shattering it into thousands of tiny pieces. Wade manipulated the walls of the caverns, creating new doorways and entrances while blocking others off, trapping the **Angermare**, keeping it away from the **Heebie Jeebies'** homes. Madam Hettyforth flitted around, working out strategies and shouting orders to the rest of the **DREAM TEAM**.

'But what should *I* do?' called Erika.

'Nothing!' commanded Madam Hettyforth. 'That thing is searching for *you*. Just stay here in the main cavern – we've got this.'

Slowly, the **DREAM TEAM** gained the upper hand. With each attack, the ***Angermare*** was forced back, deeper into the tunnels. Soon, Erika and Beastling could only hear muffled bangs and screeches as the battle continued in the distant caverns. Then an ear-splitting roar rang out and a huge section of the tunnel network collapsed. Dust billowed out, filling Erika's eyes, ears, nose and mouth.

'Heebie Jeebie?' shrieked Beastling. Erika reached out and found him in the darkness, coughing and spitting out the gritty dust.

'Silas?' she yelled into the haze. 'Wade?' But neither of them replied.

Something did, though . . . something Erika recognized. A roaring, furious something that barrelled and billowed its way along the corridor. Arriving with a screech, the ***Angermare*** burst into the chamber, an explosion of rage and greasy smoke, its eyes flickering with a furious light. Erika felt her legs weakening – her vision blurred and throbbed – she felt herself losing control. All the anger came back.

She remembered how unfair it was that Randall could do whatever he wanted, how her parents didn't want to spend time with her. As she remembered this and much, much more, a red fog descended upon her. The ***Angermare*** growled appreciatively – *this* was what it had come for.

Beastling tried to drag Erika away, but she was too heavy.

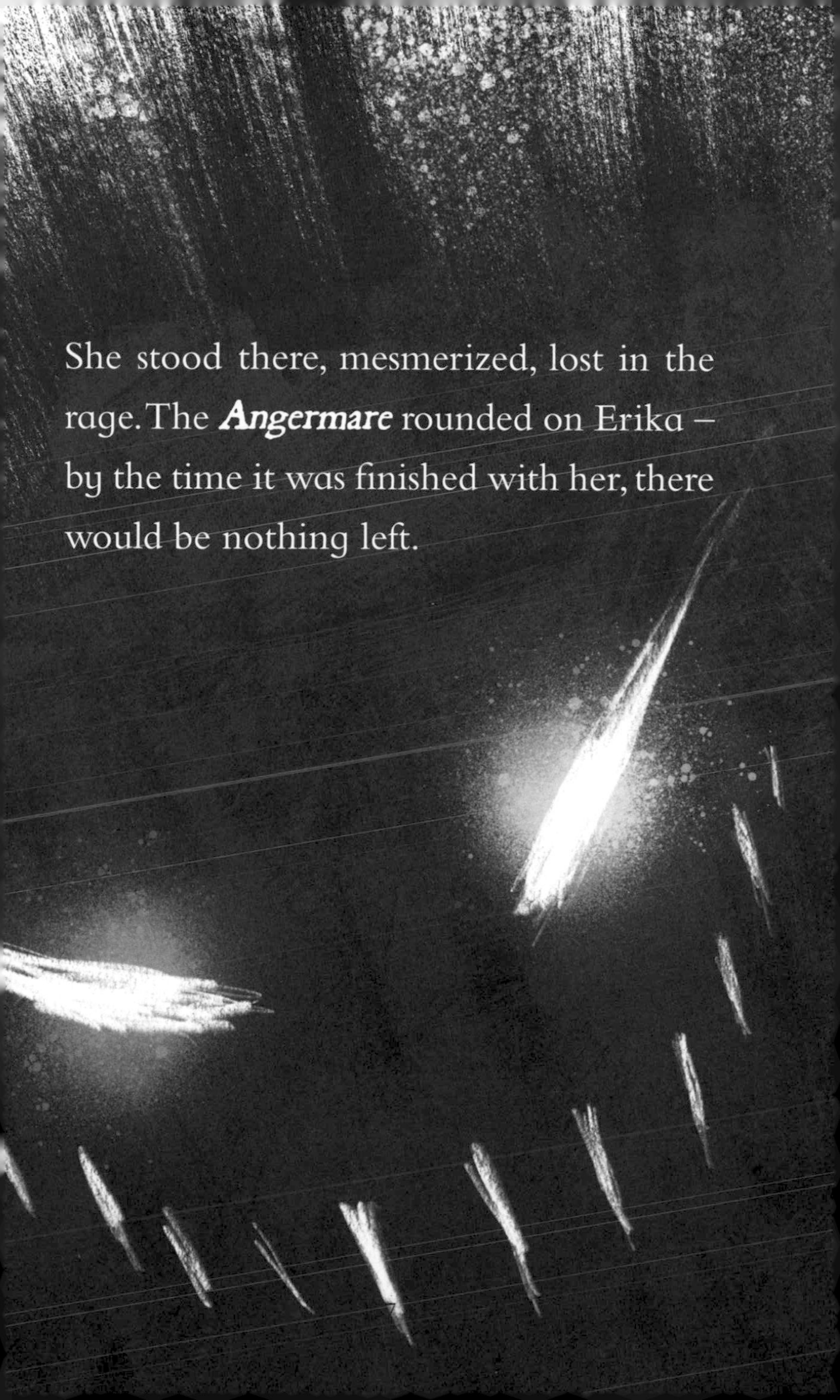
She stood there, mesmerized, lost in the rage. The ***Angermare*** rounded on Erika – by the time it was finished with her, there would be nothing left.

'No . . .' gasped Erika, struggling to get the words out. 'You *can't* make me feel like this.'

The ***Angermare*** screamed and Erika was hit with a blast of painful memories – all the times she'd been upset, offended or hurt.

'***Doesn't that make you angry?***' the voice in her head roared. '***Don't they deserve to be punished?***'

'No,' said Erika through gritted teeth. 'Why should *anyone* be punished, just because *I* feel angry?'

'***THEY MUST ALL PAY!***' screamed the voice.

Erika fought as hard as she had ever fought against the onslaught of anger. Yes, it was upsetting that Randall seemed to occupy all of her parents' waking thoughts, and yes, it did seem unfair, but how would *this* help? Deep down she knew that her parents had never *tried* to upset her, and perhaps there were things that she could have done differently too? She tried to remember happier times – to think of *anything* other than anger.

The **Angermare** hissed and wheedled. ***'You will be STRONG. You will be POWERFUL. Listen, Erika, together we can do ANYTHING.'***

A bead of sweat trickled down Erika's filthy brow and she stood her ground as the creature shrieked and roared. She could do this – *she* was in control of her anger, not the other way round.

'No!' Erika yelled over the roar. 'Some

anger *might* be useful – it can show you what you feel strongly about. But *your* kind of anger can't fix anything, it can only destroy!'

The **Angermare** shot around the room, hissing and scratching out as much light as it could, but it seemed weaker somehow.

'And do *you* want to feel like this?' asked Erika. 'Always so angry, always so upset?'

The monster roared, but it didn't sound very certain at all.

'It doesn't have to be this way,' continued Erika. 'It's a choice we all have. What's upsetting you anyway?' she asked, staring straight into the creature's eyes, which had now stopped fizzing and boiling,

'For me it was my parents. I guess I felt like they didn't want me around once they had a new baby – like they didn't love me any more – **but I know deep down that's not the case**. Perhaps if you can work out what's making *you* feel so angry, you might be able to stop?'

The *Angermare* howled, a long and piteous sound. It seemed to be shrinking right in front of her.

'Do you want to try?' asked Erika, and the *Angermare* nodded. By now it had shrunk to the size of a large dog. It still looked dangerous, but nothing like the devastating beast it had been before.

'OK!' said Erika. 'Perhaps we can help each other to work things out – does that sound good?'

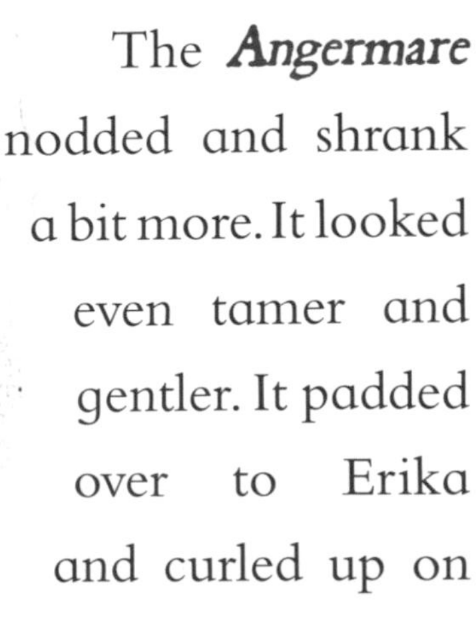

The *Angermare* nodded and shrank a bit more. It looked even tamer and gentler. It padded over to Erika and curled up on the floor in front of her, just as a huge section of the wall exploded and Silas, Sim, Madam Hettyforth and Wade burst in, yelling a ferocious battle cry.

'Gahhhhhhhh!' roared Wade. 'Let's DESTROY that thing once and for –' he stopped, looking from Erika to the tiny ***Angermare*** and then back to Erika again – '*all*?'

The ***Angermare's*** eyes flared and it bared its teeth.

'Shh!' Erika said soothingly, stroking the creature's head. 'It's OK! *It's OK!* Hi, everyone . . .' she said, smiling round at the rest of the **DREAM TEAM**. 'This is my new friend and she *doesn't* want to be angry any more. So we're going to help her, *OK*?' She looked meaningfully at the **DREAM TEAM** and nodded in an exaggerated fashion.

'O – *kaaaaay*?' said Silas.

'But . . . but . . . *what*?' whispered Wade, staring at the ***Angermare*** curled up around Erika's legs. 'How did you defeat it? The best

we've ever been able to do is drive them away, and we've had years of training!'

'I *didn't* defeat her,' replied Erika, patting the tiny ***Angermare***. 'In the end, I just tried to understand her.'

'Well!' exclaimed Madam Hettyforth, an unreadable expression on her face. 'In all my nights, I have *never* seen such a thing! But I don't think this going to be the last time that Erika Delgano surprises us.'

CHAPTER 13

After the dust had settled, Erika and the **DREAM TEAM** helped repair the **Heebie Jeebie** caves. Wade used his powers to re-form the tunnels, while everyone else did what they could to clean up.

When they'd finished, Madam Hettyforth sat down with the **Heebie Jeebie** chief to discuss arrangements for the mining of the **DREAM CRYSTAL** and how they would all work together. Erika heard Madam Hettyforth tactfully explaining that it probably *wouldn't* be possible to rename their organization **'The Heebie Jeebie Team'**, but that everyone's efforts *would* be equally rewarded.

Just before the **DREAM TEAM** were about to leave, Erika was brought to a cave filled with **Heebie Jeebies**. The chief was there and made a big show of ceremoniously sticking large quantities of fluff and a tail on to her, and then performed the strangest dance Erika had ever seen. Beastling explained that she was now an honorary **Heebie Jeebie** and would always be welcome in their caves.

Then it was time to leave. Erika whistled to the ***Angermare***, which she had named 'Marey', who scampered over and hopped into the car after her, curling up at her feet. Erika, Beastling and the **DREAM TEAM** waved out of the windows, then the car pulled away and they were gone.

As soon as they arrived back at HQ, the team hurried down to the colossal space that housed the portals into the human dreamers' dreams.

'Well, here we go!' said Madam Hettyforth as she began the process of finding a compatible dream for Erika to enter. She stood in the centre of the huge space, closed her eyes and drifted her fingers through the air as though she was feeling around for something,

'It's a bit like tuning an old-fashioned radio,' she explained as she worked. 'Where you scan across the frequencies from left to right? But in *this* case, you need to scan in every possible direction, as well as scanning through time, space and multiple different dimensions.' She paused and opened her eyes for a second, glancing at Erika. 'Actually, it's not *much* like using an old radio set, but it *is* very complicated.'

Before long, she managed to find a suitable dream and they floated up to one of the many glowing platforms that filled the space. Erika stood outside the portal to the dream, unsure what to say.

'So . . . I guess this is it, then?' she murmured, looking around at her new friends. 'Will I ever see you again?'

'Of course!' replied Silas. 'Here, take this.' He handed her a necklace with a dazzling, impossibly bright **DREAM CRYSTAL** in the middle of it. 'This is a beacon,' he explained. 'If we ever need to contact you, then we can, as long as you wear it. This isn't goodbye – I promise!' He stepped forward and put the necklace on Erika, giving her a quick hug as he did so. 'See you soon.'

'Absolutely!' said Madam Hettyforth. 'I think there are *many* ways you'll be able to help us in the future.'

Wade was standing back slightly from the group, holding on to Marey with a glowing lead made of light.

'Hey, Erika . . .' he said gruffly, 'you did well. Really well. I'm sorry if I was a bit, well, *you know* . . .'

'Miserable?' suggested Sim. 'Mean? Unfriendly? Grumpy? Cantankerous? Crabby? Argumentati—'

'All right! *All right!*' growled Wade.

'That's fine,' said Erika. 'Trust me! I know what it's like to lose your temper. Now, you look after Marey for me, OK?'

Wade nodded as Beastling leaped up and flung his arms and legs round Erika, sobbing desperately.

'Hey, hey, *shush*!' comforted Erika. 'I'll see you again soon.' She bent down and pulled him into a tight hug.

'Heebie Jeebie,' he whispered, making a tiny speech bubble that only Erika could see. It was filled with a picture of an eye, a heart and a sheep.

'I . . . love . . . *sheep*?' said Erika slowly. Beastling grinned and shook his head, the sheep became more clearly a female sheep – a ewe.

'*Ah!* Now I get it!' said Erika. 'You too, buddy.'

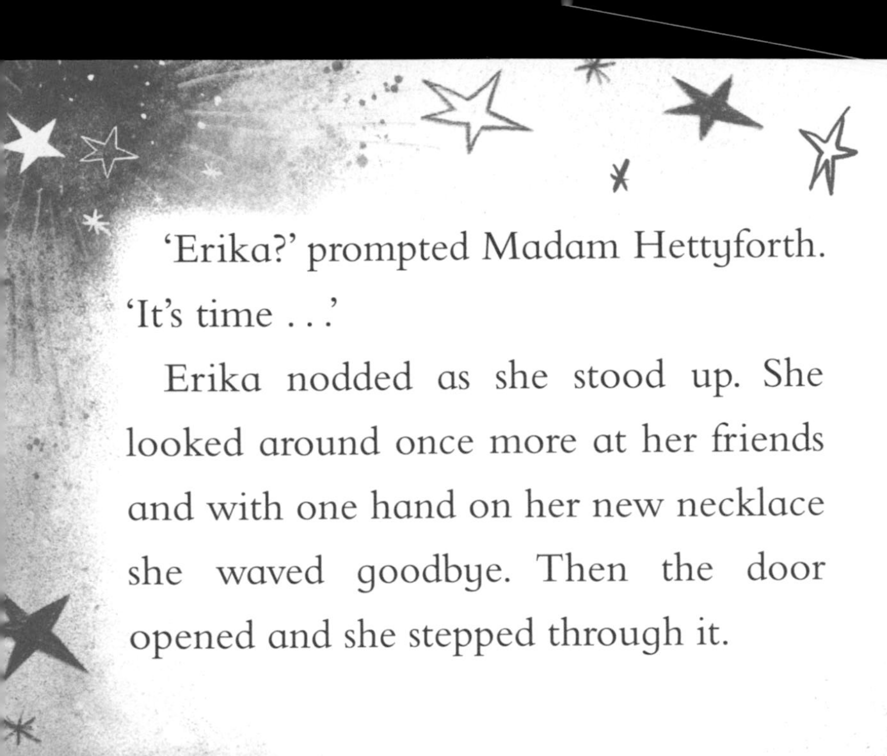

'Erika?' prompted Madam Hettyforth. 'It's time . . .'

Erika nodded as she stood up. She looked around once more at her friends and with one hand on her new necklace she waved goodbye. Then the door opened and she stepped through it.

CHAPTER 14

Erika woke up slowly. She was in her bed – *she was home.* Tears of relief stung her eyes as she looked around her room.

At first she could still feel the shape of the necklace beneath her hand, but as wakefulness washed over her she came to realize that her hand was empty. When she looked down, there was nothing there.

But it had all seemed *so* real. She could still picture Silas's expression. She could feel the warmth of Beastling's hug.

Erika swung her legs out of bed. She was forgetting some of the details of her dream already. Everyday reality crept in more and more until she began to wonder if her adventure had *really* happened. Perhaps it *had* all just been a dream . . .

'Morning, sleepyhead!' called Erika's dad as she walked into the kitchen.

'We thought you'd *never* wake up!' added her mum. 'It's nearly ten – did you sleep well? You must have been tired.'

'Yeah . . .' replied Erika. 'Something like that.'

'Nam nam!' babbled Randall, bashing his sippy cup on the table.

'He's been saying that *all* morning,' said Erika's dad. 'We've been trying to work out what he means!'

Erika peered thoughtfully at her brother. He seemed to be looking at the fruit bowl. She wandered over and picked up a banana.

'You want one of *these*?' she asked. Randall beamed a gummy smile and nodded.

'Bash!' he added. 'Bash nam nam.'

'Mashed?' guessed Erika. 'Mashed banana?'

Randall gurgled with delight and reached out two hands towards Erika. She brought over the banana in a small bowl and started mashing it up for him. She didn't get cross when he got his sticky hands caught in her hair. She didn't mind that he slopped half the banana on to the table. He didn't mean to, he was just figuring things out – like she was – like *everyone* was.

'I'm sorry I was in such a bad mood yesterday,' she said. 'I shouldn't have yelled at Randall.'

'That's OK, love,' replied her dad. 'I'm sorry we've not spent much time with you recently.'

'Yes,' agreed Erika's mum. 'We get *so* wrapped up with Randall, and it's not fair. We're a family and we need to be more of a team. Look, we'll go out today and do whatever you like. We can go into town and go to that model shop you like, or we can go to the cinema—'

'All the ice cream and popcorn you can eat!' interrupted Erika's dad, clearly getting a bit overexcited.

'I didn't say *that*!' said Erika's mum. 'But you can have *some*,' she added, smiling at Erika. 'So what's it to be?'

'You know what I'd like most of all?' said Erika. Her parents looked at her expectantly and she smiled. 'I'd like us *all* to go outside and play football in the garden. Randall can be goalie.'

'Go-wee!' shouted Randall loudly, and Erika laughed as she hugged her brother close. 'Yeah sure, "*go wee*" – whatever you like, Randall.'

It was one of those rare days when *everything* is perfect. The sun shone across the rooftops with a warm pink light as it settled in the west. Erika leaned against a tree trunk, eating the last of the takeaway pizza, while music drifted out of their living-room window.

'Do you want a hand putting Randall to bed?' she asked.

Her mum shook her head. 'No, it's OK – you two stay out here – it'd be a shame to waste such a lovely evening!'

'OK. Well, night-night, Randall,' said Erika, kissing her brother on the forehead. 'See you tomorrow.'

'Ni-ni!' replied Randall, reaching tiny fingers out towards Erika.

'OK then, Erika!' said her dad, kicking the ball over to her. 'What's it going to be? Keepy-uppies? Reckon you can do ten?'

'Easy-peasy!' exclaimed Erika, deftly flicking the ball into the air.

'Heebie Jeebie!' mimicked Randall. Erika's parents laughed at his mis-pronunciation, but Erika blinked and looked closely at her brother. She was surprised to see an unusually serious expression on Randall's face. Then her mum picked him up and carried him back into the house.

Erika yawned as she shut the bedroom door. She reached a hand up to her hair and felt twigs and bits of dried grass, so she went over to the mirror to sort it out. When she looked into the glass she was amazed to see a bright light glowing from under her oversized T-shirt. She looked down, but could see nothing there. Curious, she studied the mirror again – *and there it was*! She pulled down the neck of her T-shirt and could clearly see it – *the necklace*.

Erika reached her hands up and held the necklace in front of her face. When she looked directly at her hand it was empty, but in the mirror she could see the necklace, pulsing with a clear, brilliant light. She could *feel* it in her hand, illuminating her face, ready to call her on another adventure in the Dreamscape.

There was a tap at the door and Erika jolted round. She leaped into bed just as her dad opened the door.

'Lights out now, love,' he said. 'Thanks for a lovely day.'

'Yeah, you too. Night, Dad,' replied Erika as he bent and kissed her on the cheek. Then he switched off the lights and walked out of the room.

As the door quietly shut, Erika's dad

whispered, 'Sweet dreams.'

Erika smiled to herself – he didn't know the half of it!

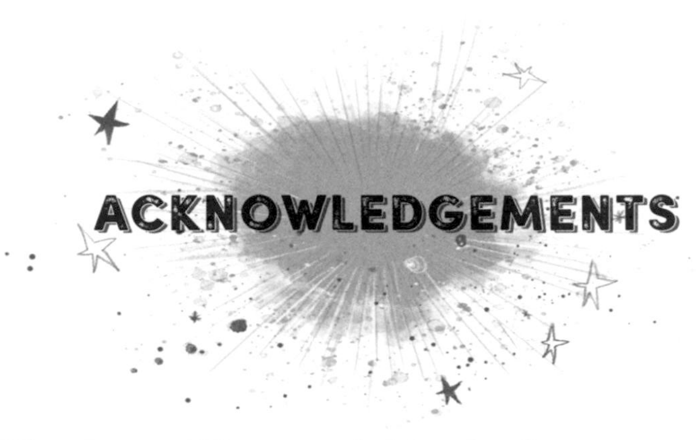

ACKNOWLEDGEMENTS

Thanks to Elinor and Mandy for top-notch representation over the years and for making sure that the Dream Team arrived safely in the hands of Macmillan Children's Books. Obviously there's a whole team of people who work really hard to make sure that these books end up being the best that they possibly can be, after all I can't print out ALL of these pages and glue them together myself, can I? Well, I could, but it probably wouldn't look very good.

I can't name everyone involved as it would take up too much space, but the Sales, Marketing, Publicity and Production departments at Macmillan all deserve some love. You heard me, big shout out to the Production MASSIVE!

Onto specifics . . . Without Lucy and Cate's judicious 'pruning' this story would still be about

70,000 words long and generally a whole lot less gooder-er than it is now. See? This bit hasn't been edited by them. This is just a taster of how terrible the whole book could have been.

Without Sue's fantastic design and layout skills the book you are holding wouldn't look half as pretty as it does and without James' vision for the cover, you probably wouldn't have picked it up in the first place. But you did! And you read right to the end, even this bit. And this bit! And I suppose that being as you've got this far, you'll probably read this bit too . . .

So finally, thanks to YOU for picking up this book and reading it, I hope you enjoyed it and HAPPY BIRTHDAY!*

T.P.

December 2019

* If it's not actually your birthday today, then just pick this book up when it is your birthday and read that last line again.

ABOUT THE AUTHOR

Tom Percival writes and illustrates all sorts of children's books. He has produced covers and internal illustrations for the Skulduggery Pleasant series, written and illustrated the Little Legends series, as well as five picture books including the Carnegie-nominated *Ruby's Worry*, *Perfectly Norman* and *Ravi's Roar*. He lives in Gloucestershire with his girlfriend and their two children.

Tom has been drawing since he's been able to hold a pencil, and making up stories for as long as he can remember. In fact, probably longer, especially as his memory is not what it once was. Basically, he's been making things up his whole life and he's not about to stop any time soon.